GR

Jake and Jill stood on the ski lodge's balcony, looking at the silver slopes and sparkling trees below them.

"It's almost too beautiful," Jake said. "Like something out of a Walt Disney movie."

"You are a cynic, Jake Randall," Jill said.

"And you are a hopeless romantic."

"I suppose so. I want real life to be like a movie, with fawns dancing around and a handsome prince kissing me in the moonlight."

"That can be arranged," Jake said, pulling Jill closer and looking seriously into her eyes. "But let's go somewhere more private—like my room."

Jill looked down at her watch. "Oh, no, is that the time?" she stammered. "Jake, I really have to go."

Jake held her at arm's length. "Sure, Jill," he said coldly. "Sure, I understand." He turned and strode away, his boots tapping on the polished slate.

On Our Own

GROWING PAINS

Janet Quin-Harkin

BANTAM BOOKS
TORONTO · NEW YORK · LONDON · SYDNEY · AUCKLAND

RL 6, IL age 11 and up

GROWING PAINS
A Bantam Book/June 1987

Cover photo by Pat Hill

ISBN 0-553-26034-0

Published simultaneously in the United States and Canada

Printed and bound in Great Britain by
Cox & Wyman Ltd., Reading

GROWING
PAINS

PROLOGUE

Dear Toni,

    Just a note to thank you for driving me back yesterday. What a crazy week we had, didn't we? I don't think anyone could have packed more into one Thanksgiving vacation. Birdbaths and mad artists and snobby actors and cute fishermen. Rosemont will seem positively dull after all that. Cassandra says she is so glad she met you—she says it's reassuring to know that she isn't the craziest person in the world! Seriously, though, she thought you were terrific, and she says she envies the relationship we have. She never really got close to anyone when she was growing up. That made me realize just how lucky we are, Toni.

    I know it seems as though we haven't much time for each other these days. Our lives have gone in such different directions, but isn't it great to know that we are still the same people? That we can still talk to each other about our dreams and worries? You know I'll always come running whenever you yell, Toni, and I hope you'll do the same for me.

In fact, our friendship was the one thing that hadn't changed during the three months I was away at college. I felt as if I was stepping into the *Twilight Zone* when I walked into my house. How about my mother? Was she as much of a shock to you as she was to me? After all those years as the Happy Housewife, suddenly she's transformed into an instant career woman. Of course I'm very happy for her, but it was a little scary. Suddenly it hit me that never again, in my whole life, would there be anybody at home to take care of me all the time. I bet you felt the same way after your dad's heart attack, didn't you? Growing up is definitely not a gradual process, as people want us to think. It hits you suddenly. One day something small will happen, and you realize that this is it—now you're an adult and nobody's going to be around to protect you anymore! It's scary, but exciting, too.

Anyway, I was really glad to get back to Rosemont. A whole bunch of kids came down to our room last night after you left. We were making so much noise that the

R.A., the resident assistant, had to tell us to quiet down. She made the mistake of starting to talk to us, and before you knew it, she was sitting there in the midst of all us freshmen, laughing as loudly as anyone. Even R.A.s are human! Then someone had the brilliant idea to have a big winter party. But the R.A. reminded us that—*finals are a week away*! That made the noise level go down instantly, without our even being asked. We had pushed the thought of finals to the backs of our minds for so long that it was a terrible shock to be reminded that they are almost here.

So for the next week do not expect any communication from me. I'll be locked in the library, trying to stuff my head full of three million interesting facts about Western civilization—Marco Polo brought back paper, gunpowder, and what else from China? Help!!—not to mention everything you've always wanted to know about the ego, id, and phobias for my psychology exam, and every book ever written for English. Sometimes I envy Cassie, taking sciences. In physics and math things are wrong or they are right. You either know the facts or you don't—not like English where I could have lots of information stored away and still flunk because Holloman doesn't like my style.

And speaking of style—there are the

small matters of the newspaper and the literary magazine still hanging over my head all the time I'm studying. We have a final edition of the newspaper to write and produce this week, and Robert and I have to make a final selection of poems for the winter edition of the magazine. Thank heavens we don't have to put it together until after winter break. The pile of poems is still depressingly small, so Robert and Cassie and I might end up having to write a dozen each or else have a two-page magazine. I don't think people will want to pay a dollar for two skinny pages of verse, do you?

I'm glad water polo is over for now. I couldn't fit that in, too. When I remember how I complained to you at the beginning about not knowing anybody and not belonging, now I feel that maybe I belong too much! I really didn't mean to get so heavily into the newspaper or the magazine, but most of the kids on the staff are seniors and they're totally absorbed in their final year. And because I have this reputation of being reliable—good old reliable Jill strikes again! Won't I ever live down that image?—everybody hands everything to me. "I'm sure Jill can handle it," they all say!

I hope I *can* handle it, Toni. Right now I'm worrying that I won't be able to get everything done in time for finals. I wish you were here. You could be my spokesperson and stop everyone from bugging me.

Can't wait for winter vacation. We get out on December 13 for a whole month. Isn't that wonderful? All those days of freedom! Actually, with Mom working, I'd better find something to do with myself. A job would be a good idea, since I can always use extra money—any suggestions?

See you soon. Behave yourself with Brandt. He is *very* cute! And I am very envious! Actually, I'm glad I'm not involved with anyone at the moment. A boyfriend would be one more complication I just couldn't handle right now. As it is, I hardly have time to eat!

Have fun signing up for your new courses!

Love, Jill

ONE

"Any more questions before we break up this meeting?" Russel asked, looking around the room from his editor's chair.

"Yeah, how come there aren't any anchovies on this pizza?" a voice from the corner growled. Everyone laughed.

"But nobody likes anchovies, Brian," Lynne answered from her perch on the arm of Russel's chair.

"I do," Brian grumbled. "Eating pizza without anchovies is like chewing on cardboard."

Jake Randall stretched lazily in a battered leather armchair. "And I say that anyone who likes anchovies on their pizza is perverted," he said. "What's more, if you don't want that last slice, I'll take it." He leaned across and pulled a wedge of pizza from the box. "Here, take a bite before I finish it," he said, leaning down to Jill who was sitting on

6

the floor beside him. Before she could protest, he had popped the slice of pizza into her mouth. "You still need fattening up since they starved you in the infirmary," he said, laughing at her surprised expression.

"Now, let's turn this discussion away from pizza for a second," Russel said firmly. "And get our schedule worked out for the final edition of the semester. We want it to be really good. We'll be publishing it four days late so we can have enough time."

Brian grinned. "I have a feeling it might be my last edition. One look at my grades on finals and I might not be asked to show up for spring semester."

"Please, let's not talk about finals," Jake said. "That's an even more distasteful topic than anchovies."

"I don't know what you have to worry about," Russel said. "You know you'll be brilliant as usual."

"Just because I study hard when all my friends are out partying," Jake said. The others exploded into loud laughter.

"When have *you* ever studied hard, Jake Randall?" Lynne demanded, throwing a balled-up napkin at him. "I can get half the girls at this college to swear that they've never seen you crack a book!"

Jake got to his feet. "If I'm going to be so misunderstood, I'm leaving," he said. "Nobody appreciates me here, except you, Jill. But then you haven't been here long enough to get corrupted, like these people." He ruffled her hair playfully as he went out.

The other faces in the room watched the door close behind him.

"You don't think he's really offended, do you?" Jill asked.

"Of course he isn't," Russel said quickly. "You have to develop thick skin now that you're on the editorial staff and attending these meetings. By the way, we didn't officially welcome you. So, welcome, Jill. Jake was bored and he wanted to leave, so he just waited for the perfect exit line. I know Jake pretty well. He's just—well, I guess you'd call him an individualist."

"It's not fair, is it?" Brian growled. "All those brains and the kind of looks that girls would kill for, too. What I wouldn't give to be able to party all night and still get an A on an exam at nine the next morning!"

Jill smoothed down her hair where Jake had ruffled it. She was still staring at the door after he had gone. She was glad to hear that other people found him hard to understand, because she had rarely met anyone who confused her so much. Since their paths had crossed in the infirmary a few weeks before she had had a couple of discussions about books with him. He was able to talk about any sort of writing, and he wrote deep, complicated poetry himself. He also had a quick wit and loved to tease people. He teased Jill a lot because he knew he could make her blush so easily. She almost blushed again then, thinking of his eyes laughing into hers as he popped the pizza into her mouth. With difficulty she turned her mind back to the discussion going on around her.

"I don't know how much help I can give you on this edition," Lynne said. "It comes out just before finals start. Be reasonable, Russel. This isn't *The New York Times*. I am not spending this last week before finals pasting a newspaper together."

"Look, Lynne," Russel said firmly, "we've all got finals. We'll just have to try. If you can just get your usual number of pages to me, that'll be fine. We'll manage to do the pasteup without you."

"Well, don't count on me," Brian said hastily. "I definitely would like to graduate from this place six months from now. And the way things look right now, that's not an absolute certainty."

"Okay, Brian, calm down," Russel said. "I'm a senior, too, you know. I have finals myself, but I'm not going to freak out over them. You just handle the sports news, and we'll manage the rest. I can do the pasteup, and Jill can get some of her freshman friends to help me. Can't you, Jill?"

Jill swallowed hard. "I guess so," she said. "But I've got to study for my own finals, so don't expect me to do too much."

"But freshman finals don't even matter," Brian said, grinning across the room at her. "Freshmen don't get kicked out because they blow their first finals. The professors just say, 'Oh, they haven't settled down yet. Give 'em time and they'll shape up.' They've been saying that about me for four years."

"You can ask Terrence Lind, can't you?" Lynne said sweetly, turning her cool gaze on Jill. "I'll bet he'd do anything for you."

Jill felt herself blushing again. *Why can't I ever react like an adult?* she thought angrily. *Won't I ever grow up so that I can act cool and sophisticated like these people? I've never seen any of them blush.* She tried to will the blush to leave her cheeks. "I'm sure Terrence will help if I ask him," she said. "Maybe Jake will help, too, if he doesn't have to cram like everybody else."

Lynne gave a sharp, brittle laugh. "Just try getting Jake to do anything he doesn't want to," she said. "He's very good at avoiding the routine, boring stuff that takes up most of our lives. Even *I* couldn't lure Jake into doing a pasteup and proofreading session."

The way she said "even *I*" made Jill instantly jealous. Lynne was beautiful, in an icy, Scandinavian sort of way. She was also very sophisticated. *Probably just the sort of girl Jake would go for,* Jill decided. *Not that I would ever want to get involved with Jake,* she thought. *I like good old reliable guys. Jake makes me too uneasy. I have a feeling that I couldn't handle a relationship with him.*

TWO

"Boy, am I glad to see you!" Jill's roommate, Cassandra, greeted her as she came back into their room.

"What's wrong?" Jill asked, nervously eyeing the dark figure who crouched on the floor surrounded by papers, black hair falling in front of her face. "Have you lost something?"

"Yes, my creative spark—if I ever had one!" Cassandra said, crawling over the papers to grab a pen from her desk. "I need your help desperately. Right now!"

"What's the problem?" Jill asked cautiously. "I've got a pile of studying to do, Cassie."

"This isn't studying," Cassandra said, pushing back her long black hair so that she could look at Jill. "This is a matter of life or death!"

"Life or death?" Jill stammered.

Cassandra nodded. "That's right. You are the

11

only person I know who can properly describe the death agonies of a tree."

"Death agonies—what?" Jill said, confused.

Cassandra jumped up from the floor. "Do you realize that they are about to start logging redwood trees in northern California—in the national parks, too?" she demanded. "Redwood trees, Jill. Do you know how long it takes a redwood tree to grow? And they're going to cut them down to make condominiums and picnic tables."

Jill fought back a smile. "That's terrible, Cassie," she said. "But I don't really see what you can do about it—unless you want to go and stand in front of the bulldozers."

"Of course we can do something about it," Cassandra persisted. "It's up to students like us to stop the destruction of our environment. Soon there won't be any trees left, Jill. There will be nothing to hold the soil in place, nothing to suck up the pollution, nothing to keep the climate temperate. Do you want to live in a parched, sun-baked desert, breathing in carbon monoxide all day long?"

Jill did smile now. "No, I don't think I would go for that," she said. "But, you know, you could be overreacting. There are laws now that prevent them from cutting down too many trees. Surely a few of them won't matter?"

Cassandra looked at her, her dark eyes wide with horror. "Have you ever been present at the death of a tree?" she asked, her voice cracking with emotion. "It's terrible. You can hear them crying out as they fall. You've got to help me stop the loggers, Jill."

"What do you plan to do?" Jill asked warily. "I don't think you could persuade me to stand in front of the bulldozers with you."

"You won't have to do anything like that," Cassandra said, her eyes pleading. "I just need your writing talents."

"But you're a terrific writer, Cassie," Jill exclaimed. "Why do you want me to do it for you?"

"I can only write poetry," Cassandra said. "But what we need here is a clear, concise journalistic style. You work on the newspaper, Jill, so you can do that. I'm designing this flyer to be put up all over campus so that we can get a busload of kids to go there and protest. But the flyer's got to make the issues very clear, and I think I'm too emotionally involved to do that. Just write the flyer for me, Jill. That's all I want you to do. Please say yes."

Jill took in Cassandra's beseeching look. She thought about the newspaper and the magazine. She glanced around the long shelf of books, waiting to be cracked for finals. She opened her mouth to say, "I'm sorry, but I really don't have any time right now." Instead she heard herself saying, "I guess I can do that much for you."

Cassandra leaped over the papers and hugged her. "You're wonderful," she said. "And you won't be sorry. Your children will thank you some day when you take them to see a redwood tree and there are some still standing."

"The way I'm going I'll be so busy for the rest of my life that I won't ever find the time to have children," Jill said, dropping her purse onto her bed and sitting down beside it.

Cassandra looked across at her. "I'm only asking you to write one page," she said. "It won't take long, Jill."

Jill sighed. "I know, Cassie. It's okay. I'm tired, that's all. And I have so much to do. None of the seniors want to work on the next edition of the paper, so it looks like I'm going to be stuck with all the grunt work."

Cassandra looked up and smiled. "You can always ask Terrence to help you," she said. "He was in here again earlier this evening, wondering where you were."

Jill smiled and sighed at the same time. "Oh, Cassie, what am I going to do about Terrence?" she said.

"What's wrong with him?" Cassandra asked, sitting down on the floor amidst all the papers. "I got the impression you thought he was nice. You certainly encouraged him."

"I know," Jill said, "and I feel so bad about that now. I *did* think he was nice. I still do. He's a good guy, and he's cute. The trouble is, I think of him as a friend. I mean, we like the same things, and all—it's just that I never dreamed he'd start feeling so strongly about me. I really can't handle a heavy relationship right now, Cassie."

Cassandra gave her a sideways look. "I would

14

think most girls would jump at the chance to get so much attention," she said. "I know I would. I'm beginning to think I'll never meet a guy who really likes me."

"Give me a break," said Jill. "What about Phil and Paul?"

"They don't really count. Most guys take one look at me and either start discussing physics or want me to help them in environmental campaigns."

"But those are the things you love most," Jill said, smiling.

"Just for once," Cassandra said, "give me a really cute guy who'll say, 'To hell with the baby seals, let's find some quiet place to be together, just you and me!'"

"Cassandra!" Jill said, laughing in disbelief. "If I report this conversation, you'll be drummed out of the Save the Everything League!"

"Oh, I didn't say I don't care about causes anymore," Cassie said. "I'd just like to find someone really special, that's all."

"Well, as I said, that's one complication I definitely don't want right now." Jill got up from the bed. "With finals and the newspaper and everything else in my life, I don't have the time or energy left for falling in love. I'm thankful that Craig and I had the sense to break up. Actually, that Craig broke up with me. I think I'd better make it very clear to Terrence that I like him, but just as a friend." She walked across the room and stood gazing out of the window at the pools of light marking the line of the road as it curved across campus. On the tower of the administration building the big clock began to chime eight. Jill looked up in horror.

"Is it that late already?" she gasped. "I promised Mr. Allen I'd be at the copy shop at eight to help him get through a big order that came in. I'd better run—I hate to keep him waiting!"

She snatched up her jacket and clattered out into the night, leaving Cassandra gazing thoughtfully after her.

THREE

When Jill arrived at the copy shop at three minutes after eight, she was gasping for breath. Mr. Allen looked up briefly as she came in but didn't seem to notice that she was late.

"So how are you this evening, Jill?" he asked pleasantly. "Nice rosy cheeks you have there. About time you got your strength back after that infirmary business."

"It's the wind," Jill said, still panting between words. "But it takes your breath away, and it stings like crazy."

Mr. Allen nodded. "Oh, yes. Rosemont always has been noted for its wind. Especially in the winter. I reckon it comes straight down from Alaska without stopping. Still, it's nice and warm in here. Why don't you fix yourself a cup of coffee before you start? You're not going to be of any use with frozen fingers."

Jill nodded gratefully and walked through the shop to the little supply closet where the coffee machine was always on. *You didn't have to run like a maniac, after all,* she told herself severely. *He didn't even notice what time it was when you came in. If you don't stop worrying all the time, you'll end up getting an ulcer!*

She came out, her hands wrapped around the warm mug of coffee. Mr. Allen, busily grabbing papers as fast as the machine spewed them out and stacking them into neat piles, did not look up. Instead he said, "Big load tonight. The students' union wants five hundred of these sets. Something about famine relief, I think. I didn't bother to read it. It's bad enough to have to get all these copies into the right order and stapled together."

"What do you want me to do to help?" Jill asked brightly.

Mr. Allen looked up. "I want you to take over, that's what. I thought I told you about my bowling team. We have a challenge game against some hotshots from Portland. I can't miss it. I told them I'd get down there by eight-thirty. Now, I've already printed everything but the last sheet, and I've got the machine all set up and running. All you have to do is take off the last page and don't forget to turn the machine off when you're through, then put the sheets in order and staple them together. There's no real rush as long as they're ready by the morning."

Jill opened her mouth, trying to form a reasonable protest. *Hey, wait a minute,* she longed to scream, *I have other things to do. I have finals and newspapers and magazines and redwood trees all crying for my attention, and you talk as if it doesn't matter if I'm here all night!* But while she was forming sentences in her head, Mr. Allen was already putting on his jacket and heading for the door. As she was about to utter a protest, she watched the door swing shut behind him, and she was left alone with the rhythmic clanking of the copy machine and the pungent smell of the ink.

"Good old Jill gets stuck again," she muttered. "Remind me to come back in my next life as a bad-tempered, bitchy, demanding person whom no one is going to ask to do anything."

She grabbed the next pile of papers before they slithered off the rack onto the floor and started stacking them, banging them angrily on the counter. The bang was a very satisfactory sound. She repeated it over and over—take papers, stack, *bang!* When she finally looked up, it came as a big shock to realize that she was not alone. She hadn't heard the door open, but then the combination of the machine clattering and her own banging had drowned out everything else.

"Terrence!" she exclaimed, the papers poised in mid-bang. "What are you doing here?"

Terrence was standing in the doorway, his blue eyes focused on her, his fair hair blown every which way by the wind. His cheeks, like Jill's, were pink, and he looked very young and vulnerable. Jill noticed his face fall as she spoke to him sharply. "Is that any way to greet somebody who's come to keep you company?" he asked.

"I don't need company right now," she muttered. "It's all I can do to keep up with these stupid papers. I only have five hundred sets to get ready before morning."

"Here, let me help you, then," Terrence said. Jill was about to tell him that she'd rather work alone, but then she noticed the look of pleading in his eyes.

"Sure," she said. "If you've really got the time. You can start stapling, three sheets to each set."

"Oh, I've got all the time in the world," he said. "Especially where you're concerned."

"But finals are almost here," Jill said.

"I know." Terrence nodded, giving the stapler such a hearty thump that all the papers on the counter jumped. "But I'm not sure if I'm going to be taking them."

"What do you mean?" Jill asked sharply, looking up from the machine. "How can you get out of taking finals? Doesn't everyone have to?"

"Everyone who's staying at Rosemont," Terrence said evenly, his eyes holding hers.

"Do you mean you're leaving college?" she asked, horrified.

Terrence shrugged. "I might," he said. "I just don't know anymore."

"But why, Terrence?"

Terrence's face flushed. "I'm not sure I belong here," he said.

"Oh, Terrence," Jill said, "all of us feel like that to begin with."

"It's not that sort of belonging I mean." He looked down at the floor. "I just don't feel I can cope with the pressure, Jill. It's just too much all of a sudden—exams and papers and everything. I keep thinking maybe I'd be better off somewhere where there wasn't all this pressure. My dad really wanted me to come here. He paid for tutoring all through high school and special tutoring just for my SATs so that I could get in. But now that I'm here, I'm pretty sure I don't belong. I'm just not as smart as the other kids."

"Oh, Terrence," Jill said, coming around the machine and reaching out to touch his arm. "I think we're all going through a panic phase just now. But I really wouldn't worry if I were you. One of the seniors told me that they don't take freshman finals too seriously here. I'm sure you'll be okay."

Terrence looked away from her and stared down at the counter. "But—but I've got all these problems, and I don't know if I can cope with them," he muttered. "Everything's piling up on me, Jill. It's not just schoolwork. I think I could keep on going if it were just that."

"So what else is worrying you?" Jill asked kindly.

"You," he said.

There was a long pause. The machine kept clanking out more copies. Jill lifted them off mechanically.

"Me?" she asked at last, avoiding Terrence's eyes. "How could I be a problem?"

"Because I'm hopelessly in love with you," Terrence said, still looking down at the counter. "I think about you all the time, Jill. I dream about you—and it's all so hopeless because I know you don't feel the same way about me." He looked up suddenly, gazing at her. "You don't, do you, Jill?"

"Well, I—" Jill stammered, embarrassed. "I like you a lot, Terrence. But right now I'm not ready to get involved with a guy again. I told you about my boyfriend, Craig. He and I were together for a long time. After you break up with someone like that—even though breaking up was a good thing—you're just left with a big emptiness. I'm not ready to feel anything for anybody else yet."

"So there's no hope for me?" Terrence asked in a small voice.

"Terrence, how do I know how I'll feel in six months or a year?" Jill asked, feeling uncomfortable. "I really like you a lot, but right now I just can't handle a new relationship. That's all I can say."

Terrence turned away and started stapling papers. "I guess I've known that all along," he said. "You were always honest with me. So it really is hopeless, then. It makes me wonder if there's any point in going on."

"Of course you have to keep on with college," Jill said forcefully. "You'd be crazy to quit just because of me."

"I didn't mean college," Terrence said evenly. "I

meant life. I really seriously wonder if there is any point in going on."

"Terrence!" Jill wheeled around sharply. "Don't talk like that."

"Well, what do I have that's worth living for?" he asked. "College means too much pressure, I'm in love with the wrong person—"

Jill came around the counter and grabbed his shoulders. "Come on, Terrence," she said softly. "We all have times when we feel really down. You're tired now. It's the end of a long semester, and you've been working hard. I feel the same way at times— like one of those little hamsters running around inside a wheel and getting nowhere. But things will get better, I'm sure. You've just got to hang in there."

Terrence slid his arms around her waist. "Will you help me hang in there, Jill?" he asked.

"I'll always be your friend," Jill said. "I can't promise more than that, but I'll be around for you to talk to."

"I suppose that's better than nothing," he said, holding her firmly in his arms.

"You go get a good night's sleep," Jill said brightly. "You'll feel much better in the morning. And I've got to get back to these papers. Look, they're starting to fall on the floor!" She reached up and gave him a quick peck on the cheek before breaking free of his arms.

FOUR

The wind slammed the door of the copy shop shut behind Jill as she stepped out into the chill night air. The wind had increased in strength since she crossed the campus three hours earlier, and now it was making the bare branches of giant trees dance crazily in the glow of the streetlights. Jill pushed her long, copper-colored hair out of her eyes and mouth and strode purposefully along the path, hearing the rhythmic *scrunch-scrunch* of her feet on the gravel. It was a reassuring sound—constant and steady. The wind at her back pushed her along so fast that she felt as if she were flying.

When she came to her dorm, McGregor Hall, the wind continued to blow insistently at her back, almost preventing her from turning and going up the steps. She kept on going past the dorm and turned onto the main road that led out of the college. Here on the exposed hillside, she met the full force of the wind. It came at her from the side now, threatening to sweep her off the pavement with every step. But she didn't slow down. She felt as though a giant bubble were about to burst inside her head. Faster and faster she walked—past the lawns, from one pool of light to the next, down the driveway between the high rows of rhododendron, almost running as the downgrade got steeper.

I've got to get away from all this, she told herself. *It's too much. Something's going to snap. Why do I always have to be the one who has to pick up the pieces? And now Terrence. I don't want to have him on my conscience, too. What if he does something terrible because of me?*

The thought made a tight knot of fear cramp her stomach so that she could hardly breathe anymore, and a pain stabbed at her side. But still she did not slow down. She kept striding through the wind— left, right, left, right, on and on, as if she could get away from all her worries if only she walked long and hard enough. She crossed the deserted highway at a traffic light and started to walk on the side near the river. The wind now smelled of water and diesel fuel, and she could hear the dark waters gurgling as they passed below her.

Suddenly a bright light shone in her face, and she nearly screamed. She stood still, panting and grasping the railing as a car flashed past, leaving a trail of red taillights behind it. For the first time, she looked around and realized where she was—down near the river on the main highway, away from the college. And it was late at night.

I must be out of my mind, she said, turning around to begin the long walk back. Only then did the danger of what she was doing really hit her—no houses within sight, no campus police patrolling the grounds, an occasional car speeding past. She started to walk faster and faster. Her whole body suddenly felt tired, and it hurt her to breathe. The wind switched direction, pushing her along from behind so that her feet felt as though they weren't even touching the ground.

Don't panic, she told herself firmly. *A few minutes at this speed and you'll be back at the entrance to campus again. There are security guards at the gateway. You'll be safe from then on. They can call one of the campus police cars to drive you back up to McGregor.* She made herself walk evenly, not run, even though her heart started to beat very fast every time a car passed.

Then, finally, the thing she had been dreading happened. She heard a car approaching, then slowing, then crawling along beside her. She forced herself to continue walking, not looking to the left or right as she strode on.

Maybe if they see I'm not interested, they'll drive away, she told herself. She forced herself to methodically place one foot in front of the other. Left, right. Left, right.

"Okay, let me guess," said a voice from the car. "You're training for the fifty-kilometer walk in the next Olympics? You're bringing the news to Rosemont that the British are coming? You're running the midnight marathon?"

26

Jill slowed to a stop and looked at the car in amazement—a little white sports car with a dark-haired figure leaning easily out of the window, watching her.

"Jake!" she stammered. "Boy, am I glad to see you!"

"I take it you'd like a ride back to college," he said, jumping out and opening the passenger door for her. She climbed in, feeling her legs tremble violently after all the walking, and sank back gratefully into the soft leather upholstery. Jake put his foot on the gas, and they shot forward.

"So, are you going to tell me?" he said at last. "I'm dying of curiosity."

"Tell you what?"

"Whether you were training for the midnight marathon?"

Jill managed a smile as he looked at her. "I just went for a walk!" she said, feeling dumb.

Jake looked horrified. "A walk—a walk along the highway at this time of night? Didn't your parents bring you up not to do dumb things? Do you realize what might have happened to you if the car that stopped hadn't been mine?"

Jill looked down at her hands. "I do now," she said. "I didn't really realize where I was going. I was angry, and I just kept on walking. When I finally calmed down, I found I was way down the highway. I don't know what made me do such a weird thing. I was lucky you came along."

Jake flashed her a wicked smile. "Of course you

don't really know me that well," he said. "Late at night, alone on a dark highway, I might not be the same lovable, trustworthy boy I am by daylight."

Jill laughed. "I never thought of you as the Eagle Scout type, even in broad daylight."

"But definitely lovable, wouldn't you say?" His eyes challenged hers. She laughed uneasily.

"So, did you have a fight with your boyfriend?" he asked. "I can't think what else would make a girl get angry at eleven-thirty at night."

"I don't have a boyfriend," Jill said. "Luckily! I can't cope with the problems I do have."

"Which are?" he asked.

"Everybody seems to rely on me." Jill sighed. "And I hate letting people down. But tonight was the last straw."

"You want to tell me about it?" Jake asked, easing the car off onto the shoulder of the road and turning off the engine.

"Well, it was bad enough when it was just the newspaper and the magazine," Jill began hesitantly. "But tonight—first Cassie and then Terrence . . ." Suddenly she found she was pouring it all out to Jake—her worries about finals, the newspaper and the magazine, her job, her roommate, and Terrence. She described the embarrassing scene with him, word for word. "So I don't know what to do about him," she said. "I can't tell him I love him when I don't, and yet—what if he left college or tried to kill himself, or something, because of me?"

Jake sat watching her, nodding as she spoke.

28

After she finished, he sat for a while in silence. Then he said, "You've still got to learn the first rule of growing up, Jill. The first rule of growing up is that you are responsible for yourself—nobody else in the entire world. If the newspaper and magazine don't come out on time, that's not your problem, unless you had personally volunteered to take over the running of the newspaper, single-handedly. Your roommate's redwood trees are not your problem, either, and neither is Terrence."

"But he is," Jill interrupted. "He says I'm wrecking his life."

Jake smiled. "Did you force him to fall in love with you?" he asked.

"No!" Jill said emphatically. "We did go out on a few dates together, but just because we enjoyed each other's company. I've tried to never treat him as anything except a friend."

"Then how can you feel responsible?" he demanded. "His feelings are his problem, Jill. You've got to learn that a lot of people in this life use guilt as a way to get what they want—"

"You don't have to tell me about that," Jill said. "My best friend, Toni, is an expert at making me feel guilty whenever I don't do what she wants. She even got me to go to Europe last summer because I knew I'd feel guilty for the rest of my life if something bad happened to her and I wasn't along."

Jake laughed. "Nobody would have to make me feel guilty to get me to go to Europe," he said. " I'd love to go. You've got to tell me all about your trip sometime."

"Sometime," Jill said. "But right now I'd like to get back to the dorm, please. I'm tired and I'm freezing and I've got a nine o'clock class tomorrow."

Jake leaned over and put his hand on her arm. "It sounds like you have too many worries for one person," he said. "You should follow my philosophy and decide that life is there to be enjoyed. Do you see me worrying?"

"You don't need to worry," Jill said. "You sail through your classes, and you know how to manage people."

"But I didn't always," Jake said, leaning back in his seat. "Believe me, if you'd known me a few years ago, you wouldn't have recognized me. I went through a terrible time when my parents were splitting up when I was in high school. For some reason I was convinced it was all my fault. I carried around this enormous load of guilt with me all the time. If they had a fight, I convinced myself it was because I hadn't eaten everything on my dinner plate or I had left the TV on. I started tiptoeing around the house, not daring to breathe in case I started another argument. I tell you, I was about to crack up. Luckily I had a teacher who noticed that my grades were getting worse and worse. He made me see that my parents still loved me; they just didn't like each other. Their fighting was their business, not mine. I watched for a few days, and I saw that it was true. After that I felt a whole lot better, and I was so mad at myself because I'd screwed up nearly a whole year at school. Don't let the same thing happen to you, Jill. I want you to promise me that starting tomorrow, you'll have the guts to say no whenever you don't want to do something. Promise me?"

"I'll try," Jill said.

"Terrific," Jake said, starting up the engine again. "Now, how about coming over to my room—I'll make us both some hot chocolate, and we can listen to some relaxing music."

"Uh, I don't think so. Thanks, anyway," Jill said. "It's really late—"

"But you need something to warm you up and relax you," Jake said.

"I really don't think so, Jake," Jill said.

"Why not?"

"Because I wouldn't feel comfortable going to a guy's room this late," Jill said. "And, anyway, you've just been drumming into my head how to say no. Now I'm practicing!"

Jake laughed. "I said starting tomorrow. And, besides, it wasn't supposed to apply to me!"

"I've got to practice on somebody," Jill said, laughing. "But I really am very tired now. I'm so glad I met you tonight, Jake. Everything you said made sense. I'm going to try really hard—I just hope I have the nerve to do it."

Jake swung the car to a halt outside McGregor. "Just follow my example and you'll be fine," he said. "You're okay, Jill. I really like you. Promise me next time you need to explode you won't go walking by the river!"

"I promise," Jill said. She opened the door and started to get out. "Thanks for everything, Jake," she said.

"My pleasure, lady," he said. "See you around, Jill!" Then he gunned the engine and roared off in a spray of gravel.

FIVE

"So, Russel, how do you want this page to look?" Lynne asked, spreading out pieces of copy over the table. "We've got the interview with the girl who swam across San Francisco Bay as the lead article, then we've got these pieces on the winter carnival and the ski club trip. Anything else belong here?"

Jill, sitting on a rickety chair across the table, tried hard to concentrate. She peered down at the various pieces of paper and tried to think of something intelligent to say. But all the time she could force only half of her mind to focus on the job. The other half was turning over facts, again and again, *The most important figures in the Renaissance were* . . . She knew that the newspaper should be finished that evening, but she was also painfully aware that her first final, in Western civilization, was only a couple of days away.

"So what do you think, Russel?" Lynne asked again patiently. "Do you want the chess club on that page or with the sports?"

Jill looked up. It appeared that she was not the only one who did not have her mind fully on the job. Russel was sitting with his head in his hands.

"Russ?" Brian asked, glancing across at Jill. "Are you still with us?"

"What?" Russel asked, looking up suddenly. "Uh, yes, sorry—the chess club, good idea."

"Good idea *what*?" Lynne demanded. "Do you want it here or with the sports?"

"Sure," Russel said. "Anywhere you like."

Three pairs of eyes stared at him suspiciously. His face looked unusually flushed, his eyes unnaturally bright. "Russel," Brian said at last, "is something wrong?"

Russel pushed his hair back from his forehead. "It's nothing much. It's just that I've been fighting off this cold, and I don't feel too good."

Lynne walked across to him and put her hand on his forehead. "Russel, you're burning up," she said. "That's no cold. You've got that flu that's been going around, I'll bet. You should be in bed."

Russel looked up, clearly alarmed. "I'm not going to the infirmary," he said. "Don't you dare tell anyone."

"But, Russ," Lynne pleaded. "If you're really sick—"

Russel shook his head. "No, I'm not going to that place. Nobody ever comes out of there alive."

"Sure they do, Russel," Jill said. "I was in the infirmary, remember? I survived."

"But there's that nurse, the top sergeant!" Russel said. "She'd make me feel ten times worse. I went to her once when I got this sliver of wood underneath my fingernail. I tell you, I was in agony, but she seemed to think I was making a fuss over nothing. She got this huge pair of tweezers and rammed them under my nail. I think her last assignment was in a prison camp. I can almost hear her saying, "Ve have vays to make you talk!"

The others laughed. "She wasn't as bad as that," Jill said.

"I don't care," Russel said. "I swore that I'd never go near her again. You guys have got to promise me that you won't take me to the infirmary, even if I get delirious."

"Okay, Russ, we promise," Brian said, getting up and helping the editor to his feet. "But you've got to get to bed and take some aspirin. Your face has turned a vivid shade of red. Besides, you're breathing germs on all of us."

"Okay, I give up," Russel said. "But you're sure you can manage without me? I don't want to let you down, when I know you're all so busy."

"We'll be fine, Russ," Lynne said. "Don't worry about us. Go with Brian, please, and get some rest. We'll all come and see how you are in the morning. We'll try to smuggle you some juice and doughnuts from the cafeteria."

"Thanks, everyone," Russel said. "You're real pals. I won't forget this. Now, you're sure—"

"Go, Russel," Lynne said.

Russel staggered out, half leaning on Brian. Lynne and Jill looked at each other.

"Men are such babies about sickness," Lynne said. "You'd think he was dying of bubonic plague instead of a simple case of flu." She smiled at Jill, and Jill smiled back.

"So I guess this leaves just us," Lynne said. "But don't worry. Two efficient women can get this job done in half the time. We'll make instant editorial decisions by the simple process of putting in anything that fits, okay?"

"Sounds good to me," Jill said. "Shall we start with this chess piece to fill up this page?"

"Why not?" Lynne asked. "There, that's page four taken care of. Elementary, my dear Watson."

For a while they worked in silence, piecing together the pages like a jigsaw puzzle.

"You know, I really don't think we should have the ski fashions right next to the piece on the football team," Jill commented, as they finished up the back page. "The football players might not want to read, 'Turtlenecks in cozy pastel angoras are definitely a must,' right next to their team photo."

Lynne giggled. "Serve them right," she said. "Always acting so macho. Let's face it, Jill. There are only the two of us, and we don't have all the time in the world. If they don't like it, that's too bad. There—that fills up the page nicely. It's not even

36

ten—that gives me three good hours for studying before my brain collapses!"

"But what about the pasteups?" Jill asked. "We still have to do that."

Lynne tossed back her fair hair. "I told Russ I wasn't doing pasteup, remember?"

"But I can't do it by myself," Jill pleaded.

"Then get Terrence to help you," Lynne said, gathering up her things and stuffing them into a large shopping bag. "Or any of your friends. It's not hard—you've done it before, haven't you?"

"Sure," Jill said. "But only with Brian and Russel here to tell me what to do."

"Well, I'm sure you'll manage," Lynne said. "Two or three of you will have it done in an hour. The stuff's all ready. It's only a question of squaring it up and pasting it down."

"So you don't think Brian will come back to supervise?" Jill asked.

Lynne smiled. "I don't think Russel will let him out of his sight. He'll probably want him to sit and soothe his fevered brow all night. Besides, Brian's the one person who desperately needs to study. He wants to get into law school, and his grades haven't been too terrific."

"And Jake?" Jill asked. "He's on the staff of this newspaper, too."

Lynne grinned. "Oh, Jake," she said. "I don't think you'll be seeing him this evening. There's a prefinals party over in Phillips Hall, and Jake has a perfect record when it comes to attending parties.

You could try going over there and dragging him away, if you want to." She turned to Jill with an amused look. "Maybe he'd break away from the festivities for you, who knows? But I wouldn't count on it."

"But that's not fair," Jill blurted out. "I have finals, too. And I care about my grades. You can't all just walk out and leave everthing for me to do! What happens if I refuse to do it alone?"

Lynne shrugged her shoulders prettily. "Then I guess the newspaper won't come out this week," she said. "Look, Jill, it's up to you if you stay or not. I am definitely going right now. I have a date with the French subjunctive, which for some reason will not stay in my head. Bye!"

Then, before Jill could say any more, she was gone.

So much for Jake's pep talk, she thought angrily. *If I followed his advice I'd say that the paper was no more my problem than theirs, and I'd walk out, too. I wonder what they'd say if I tried that. That would teach them that they can't push me around, just because I'm a freshman.* She stood for a while, poised between staying and going. *I could always say I did my share and then left*, she reasoned. *Jake's right—I've got to start standing up for myself, and tonight is as good a time to start as any.*

She started to pick up her pencils and put them back into their case. Then she flung the case back on the table. "It's no use," she said to herself angrily. "I can't just walk out. I could always get someone to help me, but not Terrence—anyone but Terrence.

An emotional scene is the last thing I need tonight, and I certainly don't want him to start feeling hopeful because I invited him to come down here and be alone with me! Hey, wait a minute—Cassie owes me a favor after those redwood trees—or maybe Robert." But then she remembered that Cassandra was out at her redwood rally and that Robert, her freshman friend from McGregor, was agonizing over his chemistry final and probably wouldn't return from the library before midnight.

She sat down and methodically began to rule up the front page. It was annoying, detailed work. Pretty soon her fingers were covered with rubber cement, and her eyes were aching from fitting the tiny squares of paper into the thin blue lines. The newspaper seemed to have mushroomed from six pages to a hundred and six.

She glanced up at the clock. Twenty minutes to twelve and still a whole back page to go! When the time came to fit in the article on the football players, it was nowhere in sight. Feeling a growing sense of panic and frustration, Jill searched the floor and the wastebasket, then took everything, item by item, off the table. Still the article didn't appear. A large blank square gaped at her from beneath the picture of rows of tough-looking guys.

"It can't just have vanished," Jill said. "It was here earlier." She remembered discussing that page with Lynne. They had talked about the football photo and the fashion piece beside it. Both the photo and the fashion piece were right where they should be. Where could the article have gone? She wondered for a moment if Lynne had taken it to play a trick on her. Surely Lynne was too mature to do a childish thing like that. But at almost midnight, Jill was ready to believe anything. In fact, she would not have been too surprised to discover that little green men from Mars had taken the article up in their spaceship with them. She started to crawl around on the floor again, even though she knew the search was hopeless.

"You really do the most interesting things late at night," said a voice above hers. "What is it now—are you in the act of worshipping some exotic Eastern god, or are you doing research on cockroaches?"

Jill looked up, banging her head on a desk as she did so.

"Oh, it's you," she said. "Great time for you to turn up. Didn't anyone tell you there was a newspaper meeting tonight, or aren't you on the staff anymore?"

Jake watched her with an amused look in his eyes as she scrambled to her feet. "I just happen to be the creative genius behind the newspaper," he said. "I don't bother myself with sordid details like pasteup."

"I can see that," Jill growled. "It seems that this newspaper is full of creative geniuses who don't bother themselves with pasteup. Otherwise, why would I be stuck here alone at midnight?"

"I thought I taught you how to say no the other night," Jake said, leaning easily against the wall and watching her. "You should have told them to get lost—or something a little less polite, maybe."

"I might have, if they'd bothered to stick around," Jill said. "Unfortunately they've all perfected the art of melting away, just the way you do. Is this something that only seniors can do? Do they teach Melting Away One as an upper-level course?"

Jake smiled. "So all the mean seniors split, and you got stuck with the pasteup, huh?" he asked. "Poor Jill. I'll have to use your life as the basis for my first dramatic novel. *The Suffering Soul of Rosemont*—how's that for a title?"

"I'm sure this is all incredibly amusing to you," Jill snapped. "But right now I'm so tired I could fall asleep on the floor, I still have a whole page to paste up, and I've lost the article for that page. So why don't you go back to your party and just leave me alone!" Her voice cracked as she spoke, and the smile left Jake's face.

"It was a boring party," he said quietly. "What do you still have to do?"

"Paste up all these stupid sports," Jill said, her voice trembling even more now that Jake was being kind. "Only I can't find my football article anywhere."

"It shouldn't be that easy to hide a whole football team," Jake said, grinning at her. "Where did you last see the article?"

"It was right under the photo," Jill said, feeling a sob lurking dangerously in her throat. "I don't know what I'm going to do. I can't rewrite that

41

article. I don't know a thing about football, and there's no way I can—" She had turned away in case she started crying and was busily rummaging through back issues piled on a shelf. She stopped talking as she heard the sound of Jake's laughter and turned to face him.

"It might be funny to you!" she said angrily. "But I've been doing this alone for hours, and I've had it up to here!" Jill drew her hand across her throat.

"Oh, Jill!" Jake said, laughing even harder. He stepped toward her. Jill backed away suspiciously. "Anyway, what's so funny?" she demanded.

"Turn around a minute," he commanded. "I think I've found your football players for you."

"You have? Where?" Jill asked, turning back toward the shelf.

"Here," Jake said triumphantly, peeling them from her jeans. "You were sitting on them. Look—some rubber cement must have gotten spilled on the article, and it stuck to you!"

"Oh," said Jill, not knowing whether to laugh or cry. "I was sitting on it. How dumb can you get?"

"Well, obviously there's something very magnetic about you," Jake said, "if that many football players get stuck on you."

His eyes were laughing as he looked at her. She started to laugh, too, in spite of herself. "Oh, Jake," she said, shaking her head in disbelief. "If you knew how long I'd been crawling around on the floor—when all the time—"

She was hardly aware that he had taken her into his arms. He held her tightly while she rested her head against his shoulder, half-laughing, half-crying, feeling the tension slip from her in the security of his embrace.

"Come to think of it," Jake said quietly, "I can easily see how it happened. I think I could get stuck on you myself."

She lifted her head to look at him, gazing into his eyes questioningly.

"I think we've always been attracted to each other, right from the start," he whispered. "We've both tried to pretend the attraction wasn't there, but it just won't go away. I don't want it to go away, Jill. How about you?"

Jill tried to speak, but for some reason she couldn't control her tongue. Instead she just shook her head, gazing up at him, feeling the powerful current she had tried to deny until then flowing through her entire body.

Jake leaned down and brushed his lips against hers. It was the lightest touch, but Jill moved back as if she had been burned.

"Don't you want me to kiss you?" he asked. "You can always practice saying no again, you know."

"I'm not sure what I want," Jill said. "I promised myself I wouldn't get involved again for a long while. I just don't have the time or the energy for a man in my life—"

"But?" Jake questioned, his eyes teasing her.

"But I guess maybe I already am involved, whether I like it or not," Jill said.

"Don't feel badly about it," Jake said. "I made myself a promise I wouldn't get involved, either. I was going to be the playboy of Rosemont all senior year. And now what happens to me? I can't stop thinking about this weird little freshman who does strange things, and I have to spend all my time rescuing her from infirmaries, dark highways, and newspaper offices. You aren't the sort of girl I'd have in mind for my playboy image!"

"Maybe you'd just better go back to your party and forget about me," Jill said. "Life would certainly be simpler that way."

"I told you before—the party was boring," Jake said, bringing his lips within millimeters of hers. "And, anyway, who wants a simple life?"

Then he kissed her again. This time the kiss was no gentle brush. When their lips parted, Jill's head was spinning.

"Now," Jake said firmly, "you and I are going to get this last page finished, and then I'm going to take you home to bed. Oh, don't worry—I intend to be the perfect gentleman. I know an exhausted person when I see one. I'll tuck you in and make you some hot chocolate, then I'll tiptoe away. How does that sound?"

"Perfect," Jill said, smiling at him adoringly. "It sounds just perfect."

SIX

"Three down and one to go!" Cassie sang out gleefully as she let herself into their room. Jill looked up from the window seat, where she was curled up with their cat, Jelly Bean, and a textbook, and smiled.

"I gather your physics exam went well," she said.

Cassie grinned. "I bluffed it," she said. "I think I invented a couple of laws that don't really exist, but I seemed to get answers that looked okay. How was your psychology exam?"

"Okay, I think," Jill said. "I pretty much faked it, too. I may have invented some phobias Freud never heard of."

"Now it's the dread English test tomorrow," Cassandra said. "Do you want me to test you this evening?"

"Thanks, but Jake said he'd come over and help me study," Jill said hesitantly.

Cassandra laughed. "So that's what he calls it," she said. "A lot of studying you were doing last time I saw you together!"

Jill felt herself blushing and turned to look out of the window. The bare winter scene outside was bathed in the reddish light of the setting sun, and the pyrocantha bushes were spilling red berries over the path, making winter look suddenly warm and festive.

"You really like him, don't you?" Cassandra asked. Like Toni, she was not always tactful, Jill decided.

"Yes, I really like him," she said, trying to keep her voice from quavering.

"*More* than like him?"

Jill hesitated. "I don't know yet, Cassie," she said. "I'm playing it very cautiously at the moment."

"I wouldn't call spending almost every minute of the past few days together playing it cautiously," Cassandra went on. "And to think this was the girl who, only a week ago, was heard to remark that she was staying away from men. 'I don't have time to get involved,' she said."

"Oh, shut up, Cassie," Jill said, turning back from the window. "Just wait until it happens to you, and then it'll be my turn to tease."

Cassandra grinned. "I just pray that you get the chance to tease me before you have to visit me in the old folks' home," she said. "I guess I'm just jealous.

I mean, he seems to have everything, doesn't he? Brains, good looks, a white sports car—"

"Cassandra!" Jill said, looking shocked. "I can't believe what I'm hearing! Is this the person who keeps insisting that material possessions are phony? And now you're starting to turn green because I've got a boyfriend with a white sports car?"

Cassandra looked embarrassed. "It's not really the sports car I covet," she said hesitantly. "It's just the image it helps to create. You know—a great-looking guy leaps into a white sports car and roars off into the sunset. It *is* rather appealing, even to a nonmaterialistic person like me."

"Cassie, we'll make a capitalist out of you yet," Jill said, laughing as she got to her feet. "But that's one of the things I like about Jake—his family is rich, but he doesn't talk about it. I mean, he drives the sports car because he needs something to drive, but he never talks about things like that. Money doesn't matter to him—not like that creep Kyle and his social-climbing friends!"

"In other words, he is perfect in every way," Cassandra said.

"He seems to be, so far," Jill said.

"And a genius as well," Cassandra said. "Doesn't that guy have finals of his own? He never seems to study."

Jill sighed. "He's just one of those lucky people who can read a thing once and remember it," she said. "He sure has helped me with my studying—in spite of those unkind words of yours, I did get a lot of studying done."

"I wish I could read things once and remember them," Cassandra said, sighing. "I keep opening these English books and looking at poems I don't ever remember seeing before—but I know I must have read them because I've written notes in the margin. The trouble is, I can't understand the notes, either."

"I feel kind of the same way," Jill said. "We covered so much in Holloman's course, and he talked so fast that my notes are a scribbled mess. But I'm hoping Jake will fill me in on some of the questions he asked in past years. I really want to do well on this exam. I mean, this is supposed to be my future major, after all!"

"I'm sure you'll do brilliantly," Cassandra said. "And Jake will do brilliantly, and then you'll get married and produce kids who win Nobel prizes."

"Oh, shut up," Jill said, throwing a pillow in her roommate's direction. "I've only just met the man, and right now I'm more concerned about getting good grades on my finals than about getting—" she stopped speaking suddenly as Jake's face appeared at the window—"I'd better get going," she finished, glancing back at the window as she grabbed her parka.

"Are you sure you don't want to study here?" Cassandra asked with no more than a hint of a smile. "I can always go to the library, you know."

"That's nice of you, Cassie," Jill said. "But you

can have the room. Jake wants to go for a little drive before we settle down to studying. He says it blows the cobwebs away. And then I guess we'll go to his room—if we can persuade his roommate to stay away."

"I know, it must be so annoying when people keep interrupting your 'studying,'" Cassandra said, with a wink.

"You'd better believe it," Jill said and flashed Cassandra a grin as she ran out.

Jake was leaning against his car, wearing a red and black buffalo-plaid jacket and looking completely relaxed as usual. His whole face lit up into a smile when he saw Jill. "So how was psychology?" he asked, pulling her toward him and brushing her lips with a kiss. "Did you tell your professor what he was suffering from?"

"That would hardly have been the way to get a good grade," Jill said. "Especially if you knew Professor Blake. He has every phobia ever listed, plus an inflated ego. But I think I did fine in the exam. Your method really works. I found I could close my eyes and see the page just the way you told me to."

"You see," Jake said, opening the door for her, "if you just do what I tell you to, you'll have a wonderful life."

"And speaking of inflated egos—" Jill began, giving him a sideways look. "How was your exam? Or was it so easy you tossed it off in five minutes?"

"More or less," Jake said. "Not easy, just

predictable. It's mostly a question of picking up on signals. If the prof mutters that something is very important or that we should make an effort to learn a thing, then you know it's going to appear on the final. I knew exactly what to expect."

"One of these days you'll be surprised," Jill said.

"Not if I can help it," Jake said. "I always like to know what to expect from life. I guess it comes down to not wanting to look like a fool."

Jill sighed. "I wish you could tell me what to expect on my English final tomorrow," she said. "You had Holloman in your freshman year, didn't you?"

Jake nodded. "And you have nothing to worry about. He'll give you a good choice of subjects, and he'll always include James Joyce and Ernest Hemingway, because they're his favorites."

"But that's terrible," Jill stammered. "I can't remember a thing about James Joyce. You'll have to teach me all evening long."

"Nonsense," Jake said. "All you have to know is that he hated and loved Ireland, hated and loved his church, and hated and loved women. There, now you've got an essay. You don't need to study at all, which means I can take you away for an evening of wild fun!" He put his foot on the gas pedal as he said that, and the bushes began to fly past in a blur. Jill was conscious of an incredible feeling of speed, frightening and exciting, all at the same time.

"Where are we going?" she shouted above the roar of the engine.

Jake raised his eyebrows and gave her a wicked smile. "We're going to a place where I always go before a stressful moment in my life. By the time you get back to the dorm, you'll be ready to face any English exam," he said.

Jill shifted easily in her seat. Why was it she never felt quite secure with Jake? She had always felt so safe and protected with Craig, but with Jake she never really knew what might happen next. The trouble was, she told herself, she liked it. It made her feel totally alive to be sitting in the half darkness beside him, speeding off to an unknown destination.

Soon the lights of Portland glowed ahead of them. They drove through the suburbs and then along the downtown streets, still busy at that time of the evening with holiday shoppers. Christmas carols were blaring through a loudspeaker, and Santa's sleigh was leaping between two department stores.

"I hate all this commercialism," Jake commented as they drew up at a stoplight. "By the time the holidays get here, I'm so fed up with Rudolph and elves and toy commercials on TV that I just want to get away and hide under my blankets until it's all over. Don't you feel like that?"

Jill shook her head. "No, I don't," she said. "I'm still like a little kid—I guess I haven't grown up yet. I love coming downstairs and finding my stocking and shaking the packages under the tree to try to figure out what's in them."

"Remind me to give you a rattle, then," Jake said, smiling at her as they drove off again. "Do you have a big family gathering?"

Jill nodded. "We always have my sister and her kids, and my aunt from Tacoma and her kids, too. We cram everyone around the table, and my dad carves the turkey—he's so slow about it that everyone dies of starvation before he's finished. But I love it. I love feeling that I'm part of something like that."

Jake looked at her wistfully. "It does sound good," he said. "I get to choose. Either my mother and her new boyfriend—you should see him, he combs his hair forward from the back of his head and sucks his stomach in when he sees you looking at him—or my father and his new wife and her two adorable little brats. The kids' first words are, 'What did you buy me?' Now can you see why I don't look forward to the holidays?"

Jill nodded.

"I plan to pass them up this year," Jake said. "I think I'll go up to our ski cabin. My older brother and his girlfriend will be up there, but it should be nice and peaceful." He pulled the car to the curb and turned off the engine.

"Where are we going?" Jill asked, looking around at the quiet shopping street.

"We are going," Jake said, taking her hand as

she climbed out of the car, "to have the best ice cream this side of the Rockies. Do you mean to say you've never heard of Big Mama's?"

Jill shook her head. "And I wouldn't have thought of eating ice cream in the middle of winter, either," she said.

Jake looked at her seriously. "To the true ice-cream fan," he said, "the season does not matter. It is a well-known scientific fact that a large helping of ice cream provides the brain with extra energy before a test. You do like ice cream, don't you?"

"Sure," Jill said. Jake led her into a bright chrome-and-glass store and sat her down at a corner table. "You wait until you've seen this," he said. "This is a Big Mama's Magic Mountain! Seven scoops, seven toppings, plus whipped cream"

"Jake!" Jill exclaimed when the waitress finally arrived with the gooey concoctions. "How are we ever going to finish this?"

"Easy," Jake said. "Just think of all the extra brain power you're digesting."

Jill laughed and dug her spoon into the whipped cream-topped mountain of ice cream and sauce. They talked and laughed and ate until their spoons were clinking against the glass sides of the dishes.

"What did I tell you?" Jake asked, laughing. "You see, you're as much of a pig as I am. In fact, we have a whole lot in common, don't we?" He reached over and touched her hand. "I've been thinking, Jill," he said, "about the vacation. Your folks won't need you at home for the whole month, will they? I was thinking that maybe you could come up to the ski cabin with me for a while."

"Wow—I don't know, Jake," Jill stammered.

"You'd really like it up there," Jake said. "It's so beautiful, Jill. Up on the hill, looking down on the lights below. There's a big fireplace, and it's very cozy. We could go dancing at the lodge sometimes. How does that sound to you?"

"It sounds great, Jake," Jill began hesitantly. "But—"

"But what?" he asked. "Don't you trust me?"

Jill shook her head. "I don't think I trust *me*," she said. His eyes, looking straight at her, were stunningly blue. "And we hardly know each other yet."

"But I want us to get to know each other better, Jill," Jake said. "How much time do we get alone in college with roommates around and finals to study for and the damned newspaper. Don't you want some time for just the two of us?"

"I do, Jake," Jill said, playing with her paper napkin, tearing at its edges and rolling it into a tight little ball. "But I don't know about our being all alone in a cabin."

"We wouldn't be alone," Jake said. "I told you, my brother would be there, and my mom is sure to come up for some of the time. There will be lots of people coming and going. You don't have to be scared."

"I'm not scared," Jill said. "But I really have to

think this over. It depends on what my parents say—maybe they'd be upset if I'm not home with them for the whole vacation."

Jake squeezed her arm tightly. "Hey, you're over eighteen, you know. You're a big girl now. You can decide things for yourself."

"I know," Jill said hesitantly. "But I wouldn't want to upset my folks or anything. Just let me think about it, okay, Jake?"

"Sure," he said, giving her his beaming smile. "You ready to go back now? I'll fill you in on James Joyce on the way home."

They drove back with Jill snuggled against Jake's shoulder. Jake didn't mention the cabin again. Instead he told her wild, improbable stories about James Joyce until she was laughing helplessly. Then, when he dropped her at her dorm, he wouldn't come in but kissed her on the porch, the warmth of his lips contrasting violently with the icy cold of their faces.

"Sleep well," he whispered, looking down at her tenderly. "And if you have to choose between dreaming of James Joyce and dreaming of me, I won't be offended if you choose Joyce."

Jill laughed as she blew him another kiss. Before she let herself in through the front door, she caught a glimpse of Terrence, standing outside near her dorm.

SEVEN

"You're back early," Cassandra said, looking up from her book in surprise. "Everything okay?"

"Everything's fine," Jill said. "Jake knew I wanted to get in early to study for my English final tomorrow. He's so considerate, Cassie. He really thinks about how I feel."

"The perfect gentleman, in fact?" Cassandra asked, raising an eyebrow.

"I don't know about that," Jill said. She walked across to her bed and started to get undressed. "He wants me to come up to his family's cabin over vacation," she added hesitantly.

"Sounds great," Cassie said. "Lucky you. Are you going?"

"I don't know," Jill said, toying with her shoelace. "I don't know about the two of us, up there alone in the snow."

"So you don't trust him to be the perfect

gentleman in his cabin?" Cassie asked with a gentle smile.

"Absolutely not," Jill said and laughed.

"So what did you tell him?" Cassandra asked.

"I said I'd think about it," Jill said. She slipped on her robe and went into the bathroom to brush her teeth. "I've got bigger worries than that right now," she said, "like a date with James Joyce in the morning. Oh, and speaking of worries, Terrence was watching us as we came in. He must have seen Jake kiss me good night on the porch. I hope that doesn't depress him even more. I suppose I'd better try to talk to him in the morning. But now I'm going to get in a couple more hours of studying."

But just as she was settling down with Hemingway, she heard her name being called outside in the hall.

"It's pretty late for a phone call," Jill said, nervously pulling on her robe again. "I hope everything's all right."

"Just another of your admirers calling to say that he can't live another minute without you," Cassandra said dryly. Jill shot her a withering look as she ran out to the phone.

"This is your long-lost friend calling," said the voice on the other end.

"Toni!" Jill exclaimed. "Is something wrong?"

"No, everything's fine. Why?"

"Because it's after ten. I always thought people only called after ten when they had bad news."

"No bad news," Toni said. "And I'm only

calling after ten because you never seem to be in at any other time."

"Yes, well—" Jill began.

"I guess you must be spending all that time in the library, studying," Toni went on before Jill could answer. "I know how hardworking you are before exams. That's why I called, partly. I wanted to wish you luck on your exams."

"That's really sweet of you, Toni," Jill said. "And your timing is very good, because tomorrow is the exam I really need luck for. It's my English final—a three-hour essay for Dr. Holloman."

"I'm sure you'll do fine," Toni said. "You know you write brilliant essays. I always got an A when you wrote mine for me."

"But that was high school," Jill said. "And it wasn't for Dr. Holloman. He deducts points for every little thing and writes things like 'trite' and 'cliché' all over the margins. I really want to do well on this one, so I can come home and relax."

"That was the other thing I wanted to talk to you about," Toni said. "You do get out the thirteenth, don't you?"

"That's right. Only two more days and then freedom! Actually I could leave tomorow after English but I need to pack and get organized."

"Do you have any plans for the vacation?"

"Not exactly," Jill said hesitantly. "Did you have something in mind?"

"I might have," Toni said. "I might have

something that would be a lot of fun. I just wanted to see if you were free first."

"What is it?" Jill asked impatiently.

"I am not at liberty to disclose any more at this time," Toni said. "Oh, did I mention I'm thinking of going into politics? I've signed up for a political science class. Anyway, I may have some news tomorrow, if you're interested."

"Toni—how can I say I'm interested when I have no idea what you're talking about?" Jill said impatiently. "I might be committing myself to an expedition to the Antarctic or nude dancing in Las Vegas, knowing you."

"It's more fun than either of those, and it'll make you a lot of money," Toni said.

"Is it legal?"

"Very legal."

"Well, I sure could use the money," Jill said. "Now I know I'm going to spend my whole English final wondering what it is."

"Well, I thought you might need cheering up this vacation," Toni said. "After all, Craig's not going to be hanging around anymore, so I thought you might be feeling lonely."

"You're not trying to fix me up with a date, are you?" Jill asked suspiciously. "Because the last thing in the world I need is more complications with men!"

"But they *are* fun to have around," Toni said. "Though the answer is no, I'm not trying to fix you

59

up with a date. I learned my lesson after that horrible actor I got for your blind date. I'm trying to fix us both up with a fun job, that's all."

"In that case, it sounds like a great idea," Jill said. "And it would take care of a major complication in my life right now."

"Some guy is chasing you, but you aren't ready for a heavy relationship yet?" Toni asked.

"Something like that," Jill said, not wanting to go into more detail over the hall phone. "I'll tell you all about it when I see you in three days."

"Terrific! I can't wait," Toni said. "I've missed you so much."

"Ha!" Jill said. "With Brandt hovering around all the time, I doubt you've even noticed I'm gone."

"But it's not the same," Toni said. "I can tell you things I could never tell Brandt. And he's not around all the time. I know that I have to play second fiddle to his crummy plays. But I guess he's worth waiting around for. He's going to be away over the holidays, by the way. He's helping a friend of his direct a movie, lucky thing."

"Oh, I get the picture—no pun intended," Jill said. "You only want me home because you'll be lonely without Brandt."

"Who said anything about being home?" Toni asked mysteriously. "If things work out well, we'll both be away."

"Away—where?"

"I am not yet at liberty to disclose—"

"Oh, shut up. You can be so infuriating sometimes. But I don't know about going away, Toni. My folks might feel bad about that."

"I doubt it," Toni said. "I met your mom when I was home visiting my mom and dad, and she said she was going to have to work overtime for the next few weeks. She said she felt bad that you'd be left on your own so much. In fact, she was even thinking of quitting her job so that she could spend more time with you."

"But she can't do that," Jill said emphatically. "She loves that job. It's the best thing that's happened to her in years. Oh, Toni, it looks like you may be dragging me into another of your fiendish schemes after all."

"Great," Toni said. "I wouldn't have wanted to go alone. Now I just hope it comes off. I'll call you tomorrow, Jill. And good luck on your exam."

"Thanks. I'll need it," Jill said. She hung up the phone and walked back down the empty hall.

EIGHT

Jill stepped out into the midday sunshine and heaved a sigh of relief. She had survived the English final. Not only survived—she had a feeling that she might have done well. The big essay question had been on heroes and anti-heroes, and, thanks to Jake, she was able to write knowledgeably about James Joyce and Ernest Hemingway.

As she paused to breathe in the crisp winter air outside the stuffy classroom, she watched Terrence emerge from another class, blinking like an owl in the bright light. *Should I say anything about last night?* she debated. *And, if so, what in the world should I say?* Thoughts flashed through her mind: *I know it looked as if I was giving someone a passionate good-night kiss, but I was really only saving his lips from frostbite—whispering a long secret—noticing he was about to faint and administering instant mouth-to-mouth resuscitation. . . .* Jill felt her lips twitching into a grin. *You're reacting to the stress of a final by going crazy,* she told herself. *Just act friendly toward him. You don't have to explain anything.*

She turned and smiled at him. "My exam wasn't too bad. How was yours?" she asked.

Terrence gave her an icy stare and strode off ahead of her. Jill watched him for a moment, then ran to catch up with him. "Look, if something is bothering you, why don't you come out and say so?" she asked, taking giant steps to keep up with him. "Have I done something to make you mad?"

He gave her another stare, icier than the first.

"Terrence, you're acting childish," she said. "I thought we were friends. Are you mad because of last night?"

"Oh, no," he said, staring straight ahead as he walked. "Why should I be mad? After all, it was dumb of *me* to believe you when you said you weren't ready for an involvement yet. What were your exact words? You didn't have time for a man in your life? Of course, I suppose I don't qualify as a man. After all, I'm not a senior who drives a sports car—"

"Terrence," Jill said angrily, "it's not like that at all. Do you think I'd go out with a guy just because he was a senior or had a sports car? You don't think that little of me, do you?"

Terrence looked at her, raising an eyebrow. "So how do you explain the fact that one week you're swearing off men and the next week you're all over

63

some guy who happens to be a senior with a sports car?"

"Look, Terrence," Jill said patiently, "you don't choose who you fall in love with, do you? You should know that—otherwise you'd never have picked me."

"You're telling me you're in love with Jake Randall?"

"I guess it's a bit premature to say that, but I'm attracted to him."

"Even though he has a reputation for being the biggest playboy on campus—or maybe *because* of his reputation?"

"I don't care about reputations," Jill said. "Jake is very nice. He likes me, and I like him. That's all I can say." On impulse she reached out and touched Terrence's arm. "Listen, Terrence, I didn't plan things this way. Jake and I met, and it just sort of happened. I really like you, but I can't flip a switch and turn on something that isn't there. I don't feel that way about you. I don't want you to think badly of me because I can feel that way about Jake."

Terrence turned away from her. "I just don't want you to get hurt, that's all."

"I'm a big girl now," Jill said softly. "I can take care of myself, and I don't intend to rush into any relationship. But I have to make my own choices. They always say, 'If you love something, set it free,' don't they?"

Terrence managed a smile. "I suppose they

do," he said. "Is that a polite way of asking me to butt out of your life?"

"Not butt out, Terrence. I really like having you as my friend. But I want to live my own life and make my own mistakes," Jill said.

"Okay, wise lady," Terrence said. "I know you're right, and I know that you're a terrific person. That's what makes it all so hard for me. I could stop thinking about you so much more easily if you were mean and evil."

Jill smiled back at him. "You don't have to stop thinking about me, but you can practice over the vacation thinking about me as a friend. I want you to have a great vacation and fall madly in love with a terrific girl. That's an order, understand?"

"Yes, ma'am," he said, saluting. Then he smiled wistfully. "I'll try, Jill. Will you write to me sometime?"

"Sure I'll write to you," Jill said. "And I want you to write to me, too. I'm dying to know your psych grade. Have a good vacation, Terrence, if I don't see you before we go."

"And you, too, Jill," Terrence said.

He turned toward his dorm and loped up the steps with long strides, leaving Jill staring after him. She shook her head and walked on toward McGregor, feeling vaguely confused. She had seemed very confident when she was talking to Terrence, but now that he was gone the doubts that had been circulating in her mind reappeared. What did she really feel about Jake? Was she just attracted to him because he was a very good-looking senior with a sports car? She remembered seeing Lynne's face stiffen when they passed her on campus, walking hand in hand. That was definitely part of the attraction. And then there was his reputation: was she also attracted to him because he was different from all the reliable, steady boys she had dated in the past?

But it's not just those things, she argued with herself. *I like him. I feel good when I'm with him. He makes me laugh and relax. And he does care about me.*

All the same, it was true that he switched girlfriends as often as most people checked out library books. Jill knew how easily she could fall in love with him and she also knew how much it could hurt afterward! *Better play it safe over the holidays,* she thought. It would be terrible to get really involved with Jake and then come back to college to find that he had already gotten tired of her and moved on to a new girlfriend. *If Toni's scheme does come off,* she decided, *it will give me an ideal excuse not to go to his cabin!*

She let herself into McGregor and took down the note that someone had taped to the message board outside her door. "Jill—Someone called Toni has called three times and says you must call back instantly. Matter of life and death."

Jill smiled as she hurried to the phone. If they only knew what Toni considered to be matters of life and death! She dialed Toni's number.

"Where were you?" Toni demanded as soon as she came on the line.

"Did you forget the small matter of one English final?" Jill asked sweetly.

"Oh, I know all about that," Toni said impatiently. "But you said it got out at noon, and now it's nearly twelve-thirty."

"I did have to collect my stuff and walk across campus," Jill said. "And I had to talk to someone for a few minutes. I didn't realize I was supposed to sprint back, just in case my friend from Seattle called."

She heard Toni's giggle on the other end of the line. "Well, you know what I'm like when I've got news. I can't wait two seconds."

"Okay, so tell me the news," Jill said. "I must admit, I'm curious."

"We got the jobs," Toni sang into the phone so loudly that Jill had to hold the receiver away from her ear. "We can start next week!"

"Are you now at liberty to divulge what kind of jobs we have? I'd like to know whether to show up wearing my oldest jeans or my prom dress or even my bathing suit!"

"These are the most terrific jobs in the world, Jill," Toni said. "Just imagine—they've opened this new ski resort, and we're going to be working there!"

"But, Toni, what you and I know about skiing is nothing. What on earth did you tell them we could do?" Jill asked very suspiciously.

ON OUR OWN

"Oh, we're not going to be working on the slopes, dummy," Toni said. "We're going to be in the new luxurious lodge, mingling with the guests, livening up the après-ski, cheering up all the lonely, good-looking guys—"

"Toni, are you telling me we're going to be paid to mingle with the guests?"

"Well," Toni said reluctantly, "we *are* going to be expected to help out with some of the house-keeping chores. You know, empty the ashtrays, clear up the rum punch glasses—whatever needs to be done. But think of what we can do in our free time—all the mingling we want, dancing in the disco all night, skiing free all day. Doesn't it sound exciting?"

"It sounds almost too good to be true," Jill said hesitantly. "What about your job at the theater?"

"Well, since I didn't get my week off at Thanksgiving, I get a month off now, too!"

"How long is it for?"

"Until after New Year's, I think. That's the busy season."

"I don't know about being away for Christmas, Toni. I kind of look forward to Christmas at home—"

"It's not that far," Toni said. "You could take Christmas Day off and get a ride down easily. Come to think of it, I'd like to be home for Christmas, too. I'll talk to Mr. Swensen about it when I tell him we're accepting—"

"Hey," Jill interrupted. "I didn't say I was

68

taking the job yet. I'm not completely sure about leaving my folks—"

"But I told you your mother was going to be extra busy until Christmas," Toni pleaded, "and if we finish after New Year's, you can still have more than a week at home. And think of the money, Jill. We get free food and free lift tickets and all sorts of goodies. We'll be able to save everything we earn."

"I sure would like to save some money," Jill conceded. "How did you find out about this, and how come we got the jobs?"

"Oh, let's just say I had my ear to the ground. Most people don't even know this place exists yet. It only opened over Thanksgiving this year, so we were just lucky, I guess. So, are you excited? Are you going to go with me?"

"It does sound great," Jill said slowly. "And it really would make my vacation a lot less complicated."

"So I'll call Snowfire and tell them we'll be there on Monday, okay?" Toni asked.

"All right," Jill said. "You can tell them we'll be there."

On the other end of the line Toni gave a great yell of delight, which caused a deafened Jill to hold the phone away from her ear.

"I only hope I'm not letting myself in for another of your crazy schemes, Toni Redmond," she muttered as she walked away from the phone.

Late that afternoon she met Jake. She sat uneasily beside him in the car as they drove out along the river.

"I thought we'd go out and celebrate the end of finals and the beginning of vacation tomorrow," he had said when he came to pick her up. "A long drive, a really fancy restaurant—how does that sound?"

"Sounds great," she had said, looking at him and noticing how incredibly handsome he looked. Jill only had to look at Jake to see that he enjoyed life to the fullest. And when she was with him, she felt happy just to be alive. *It would have been such fun to go up to his ski cabin*, Jill thought wistfully. *But I promised Toni. I can't let her down now.*

After a while Jake parked the car beside a cliff and helped her out. "I want to hike up to a waterfall," he said. "The view is magnificent, and we should be able to make it to the top before the sun sets."

"But, Jake—I'm not dressed for hiking," Jill protested, looking down at her long, soft wool skirt, her high-heeled boots, and her oversized wool coat.

Jake gave her an encouraging grin. "It's all paved," he said. "Just a lot of steps. And, besides, I want you to get your legs in shape for some intensive skiing. I don't want to win all of the races we're going to have."

Jill took a deep breath. Now was the ideal moment to tell him. "Uh, Jake," she said hesitantly.

"About the vacation—I—I can't come up to the cabin."

He turned and looked at her, his eyes suddenly dark. "You can't, or you don't want to?" he asked quietly.

"I do want to," she said. "I really do. It's just that—well, several things. I need to earn some money over the vacation. That's a number-one priority. My parents really can't afford Rosemont, and I want to do my share. Then there's my best friend, Toni. I told you about her. She's found a terrific job up at the new Snowfire Ski Resort. I can work there, too. In fact, she won't go without me. We've been friends all our lives, Jake. I can't let her down. So if you want to ski with me, I guess you'll have to come up to Snowfire."

She uttered this last sentence lightly, but her voice quavered. Jake took both of her hands and held them firmly. "Hey, it's okay—I think I understand. Don't worry about it," he said. "If you have to work, you have to work. And you might as well work somewhere fun, rather than putting in four weeks at McDonald's. You just have to promise me that you won't meet any cute guys up there."

Jill gazed up at him and smiled. "I promise," she said. "I'll walk around with a veil over my face all the time if you want."

"Oh, no," Jake said firmly. "You'd look much too cute with those big eyes peeping out over the top of a veil. How about a grocery bag instead?"

"Okay, a grocery bag, if you insist," she said.

He laughed and dragged her up the path. "Listen," he said, as they walked, "I was only joking. We've just met each other. I have no claim on you. If you meet someone over the holidays, that's up to you."

"You don't have to worry," Jill said. "I told everyone a couple of weeks ago that I didn't want any complications in my life this year, and I've already got you. That's about all I can handle."

"Thanks a lot," Jake said. "You sure know how to boost a man's ego."

"But you're a very nice complication," Jill said, turning toward him. Jake didn't need any more encouragement. He took her firmly in his arms and began kissing her, holding her very close and crushing her lips against his.

"Jake," Jill whispered at last, "we're on a public path. Anyone could see us!"

"Let them see," Jake whispered back. "Might give them a few lessons in technique." He began kissing her again, this time so demandingly that Jill forgot to protest.

When he finally released her, they climbed, arms entwined, up the last few steps. They stood above the valley with the roar of the waterfall beside them, silently watching as the river below them turned from pink to silver as the sunlight faded. Then, still without talking, they made their way down again.

I must be crazy, Jill thought as they saw the car

below them, *to turn down a chance to go to his cabin with him. I can't think of anything I want more.* Then she checked herself. *Are you forgetting who you are?* she asked herself severely. *You are sensible, reliable Jill Gardner. You do not run off to lonely cabins with boys you have only just met. If Jake really cares about you, if he feels the same way you feel about him, he'll still be around after winter break, and things can progress from there. Nothing good ever comes from rushing into things.*

But as they parted that night, she wondered if she had made the biggest mistake of her life and lost him forever.

NINE

"Tell me again about this glamorous ski resort," Jill said, looking up and pushing her hair out of her eyes with a soapy hand. "You know, all that stuff about the great après-ski life and mingling with the good-looking male guests."

Beside her Toni only grunted and stuck her arms deeper into a sinkful of greasy water. "Because," Jill went on, "I'm still waiting to find out about it. So far all I've seen of the glamorous ski resort has been a lot of swirling snow as we came up, then the wall of a bedroom and the wall of a bathroom and the wall of a kitchen, none of which I would call glamorous. And as for mingling—if you don't count the bellboy who showed us to our rooms last night, the only mingling we've done so far has been with Heavy Hilda. And I am not at all sure I want to continue that relationship!" Heavy

Hilda was the name the girls had given to Mrs. Hansen, the portly kitchen supervisor.

"We've only been here a day," Toni snapped. "So it's not really fair to judge anything yet."

"So you do admit," Jill insisted, "that so far it hasn't been glamorous for you either?"

Toni looked up and nodded. "But it will get better," she said. "They said they were having problems with the dishwasher today, that's why we've been stuck down here. As soon as they fix it, I'm sure they'll give us better things to do, and then we'll get some time off."

"Are you sure?" Jill asked. "Have you seen it in writing?"

"Don't be dumb," Toni said angrily. "Everyone gets time off. It's the law. Only slaves have to work every day."

"And you're sure you didn't sign us up as slaves?" Jill asked icily. "Because Mr. Swensen seemed to be hinting that you told him you'd do anything to get this job. Is that correct?"

"Look, why are you attacking me like this?" Toni asked, exploding as she always did when she had been pushed too far. "So we're washing dishes right now—"

"We've been washing dishes all day," Jill reminded her. "And this kitchen is very dark and gloomy."

"But we're getting paid for it," Toni said. "And we'll be able to meet people on our days off."

"I don't believe it," Jill said grouchily. "I bet Heavy Hilda comes to chain us to the kitchen wall overnight."

Even Toni had to giggle at that.

"I mean—honestly, Toni," Jill said, suddenly starting to laugh as well, "isn't this like something out of a bad Gothic novel? Two young girls stuck in an underground prison, water pipes clanging over their heads. The girls slave away scrubbing pots and pans because the dishwasher has broken down on their first day on the job, hearing the faint sounds of music and laughter above them while this ogre of a woman seven feet tall and six feet wide, with a black moustache, walks behind them cracking a whip?"

Toni giggled harder and glanced around to see if the kitchen supervisor was out of earshot. "She is pretty terrible," Toni admitted. "But it's got to get better. If not, I'll complain to Mr. Swensen."

"I don't see what good that will do," Jill said. "From what I heard, you convinced him that we loved hard work and we'd do anything to get this job. What exactly made you say those things? Do you have one of your crazy reasons for bringing us here that I don't know about yet?"

"Of course not," Toni said. "I just thought a new ski resort sounded like fun—and we both needed a little break—"

"For your information," Jill said, "I could have had a very good break up at a ski cabin with one of the cutest boys in the West. I turned it down to be with you, washing dishes at eleven o'clock at night."

"Why did you do that?" Toni asked. "If that had been me, I would have gone like a shot. Who is this guy?"

"Jake Randall," Jill said. "I think I pointed him out to you once when you were down visiting. Remember I told you that he wrote great stories?"

"Is he tall, dark, and handsome, with a lean and hungry look?" Toni asked.

"That's the one."

"You should go see a shrink!" exclaimed Toni.

"That's what I'm telling myself right now," Jill admitted. "But at the time I didn't want to let my best friend down, and I thought I might have a good time up here, too."

"Gee, I'm sorry, Jill," Toni said, pushing back a blond curl and leaving a soapy blob on her forehead. "You shouldn't have done that for me. Is it too late to call him and say you're coming after all?"

"What, and leave you here to cope with Heavy Hilda on your own?" Jill asked. "Or do you want to quit, too?"

Toni shook her head vehemently. "Oh, no, I'm not quitting," she said. "Never let it be said that a job got the better of Toni Redmond. I'll stick it out until the bitter end, telling myself all the time that it's got to get better."

"Then I guess I'll stick around, too," Jill said. "I don't want you to think that I give up before you do. Here, pass me that lasagna pan. My water's much hotter."

As Jill scrubbed away at the baked-on crust of

dried pasta and burnt cheese, she thought about what they had just discussed. Would she really stick it out here for three weeks, stuck in a dank kitchen, up to her armpits in grimy water, just for Toni? She had been working so hard all semester—didn't she deserve a better vacation than this? *And why is Toni so desperate to be here,* she wondered, glancing across at her friend who was stacking soapy plates for rinsing. *I'm always suspicious when she arranges something crazy like this. Usually she has some plan up her sleeve. And all I have up my sleeve at the moment is tepid, greasy water!* She looked down at a piece of burnt cheese floating around like a miniature island. *If Jake could only see me now,* she thought, not knowing whether to laugh or cry. A daydream slipped into her mind: Jake showed up, pushing Heavy Hilda aside and sweeping Jill away to a warm, comfortable, romantic ski cabin. With an effort she switched off the daydream. *But I don't want to be at a cabin with Jake—I've already decided that,* she told herself firmly. *I know I couldn't handle that situation. At least I'm comfortable here with Toni.*

Then she realized her choice of words hardly described her present situation. Was this comfort? Her hands were cold, a draft was hitting the back of her legs, and her feet were sore. Comfortable, she decided, was their living room at home—a cozy, warm living room, with soft armchairs and a big fire. *I could have been there right now,* Jill thought and instantly felt a twinge of guilt as she remembered her conversation with her mother.

"So you won't be at home at all this vacation?" her mother asked when Jill had called to tell her about the job.

"I'm going to make sure I'm home for Christmas Day," Jill said brightly. "And I'll have about ten days from the third on. Anyway, Toni told me you were going to be sort of busy—"

"Well, that's true," her mother had said. "And I can understand, dear, that you wouldn't want to be alone at home all day. You just kind of took me by surprise, that's all. Of course you must go, Jill. I'm sure Toni wouldn't want to be there without you, and it will be a lot of fun. But do make it for Christmas. It wouldn't be the same without you."

"I'll miss you, too, but I do need the job. And I'll be home a little later, Mom."

"I understand, Jill. You go and have a good time," her mother said. "We'll make the most of you after New Year's. I'll try to get some time off from work then, and we'll go shopping and I'll bake some cookies, okay?"

Her mother had sounded bright and encouraging on the phone. But when Jill had gone home for a day to pack her bags for the mountains, she knew how much her mother would miss her. *Maybe I should have stayed home*, Jill thought. *Maybe I'm not being fair to my folks. It's so hard to please everybody.*

"Aren't you two girls finished yet?" demanded a booming voice from the doorway. The sound of the voice reverberated through the huge, cavelike kitchen. Jill and Toni turned around cautiously. Mrs.

Hansen stood there with her hands on her hips, glaring at them out of her small, piggy eyes.

"We still have these lasagna pans to do," Toni said. "They're a big mess, with cheese and sauce all burned onto them."

"Well, get a move on," Mrs. Hansen urged. "I'm waiting to lock up and get out of here."

"We're working as fast as we can," Jill said. "You're lucky we arrived last night, or you'd have had to do all this yourself."

Mrs. Hansen grunted and walked away again.

"Good for you," Toni said in a low voice as Mrs. Hansen left. "You really told her. You're beginning to sound more like me all the time. I think college is doing you a lot of good."

Jill smiled. "Well, I've gotten used to speaking up to Dr. Holloman, so I'm certainly not going to be frightened by that overbearing woman. Isn't she the most revolting person you've ever seen?"

Toni looked back and considered. "Maybe not the most," she said, "but *one* of the most, definitely. And one of the fattest, too."

Above their heads the band struck up a new number. They could hear the rhythmic thump of the bass vibrating through the floorboards and snatches of singing, too faint to recognize. There was a sudden burst of laughter as a group of people passed by the top of the stairs.

Jill turned to Toni. "Well, at least now we know what Cinderella must have felt like," she said.

"Exactly," Toni agreed. "All we have to do is sit back and wait for Prince Charming to rescue us!"

TEN

The next morning Jill awoke to the eerie blue light reflected off the snow outside. For a moment she lay there, trying to identify the unfamiliar objects in the room. The narrow white closet and the cheap brown chest of drawers did not belong to her room at college, nor her room at home. It was only when Toni sighed and turned over in the bed next to hers that Jill remembered where she was: at the ski resort. Then every muscle began to ache as she remembered standing in front of a sink for ten hours straight.

I wonder if it's still snowing outside, she thought and sat up. She instantly regretted emerging from the warm nest of her bed: their tiny room in the staff quarters was not nearly so well heated as the main lodge, and an icy blast of air hit her head and shoulders. She grabbed her quilt and pulled it around her as she crossed to look out the window at the sparkling scene outside. Right next to their window a huge pine tree was draped with a glistening white blanket of snow. Beyond it rose the pristine whiteness of a hill with the sun already peeking over it. After the heavy snowfall of the day before, most of the smaller shapes were unrecognizable—just humps and bumps where fences or garbage cans might be hidden. At the edge of the roof a row of icicles caught the first rays of sun, and the only sound was the rhythmic drip as they melted.

Suddenly the prospect of three weeks at the lodge didn't look so bad. The session the night before in the kitchen seemed no more than a bad dream. She had the feeling that Toni was right: things were going to get better. She thought happily about the fact that she had four weeks of vacation ahead of her, chances to go skiing and dancing. She might make some new friends, and she would go home with a little money. Best of all, there was the picturebook snow scene outside, almost magical in its beauty. Jill looked across at Toni's bed. "Wake up, sleepyhead," she said, reaching out of her vertical cocoon to prod the inert lump of bedclothes. In response came a grunt, then silence.

"Come on, it's a beautiful day and the sun is shining!" Jill pleaded.

Another grunt. Jill grinned and waited patiently. "Okay, go back to sleep if you want," Jill went on. "I'm sure you won't mind missing breakfast before we report to Heavy Hilda!"

This pronouncement of doom obviously got through the layer of bedclothes because Toni sat upright with a surprised look on her face, then uttered a horrified yell.

"It's freezing in here," she stated and immediately disappeared under the covers again.

"It's warm in the bathroom," Jill said sweetly. "And I'm going to get there first and use up all the hot water for my shower." Toni jumped up, shot across the room, snatched her robe as she passed, and disappeared into the hall. "Beat ya!" she called triumphantly as she slammed the bathroom door. Jill shook her head and smiled. As always, Toni was unsquashable. Jill wondered if anything could keep Toni down for long. She romped through life as though it were one long, challenging game and as if each day held the promise of new adventures. *Without her around I would have turned out to be a very different person*, Jill decided as she chose a ski sweater and faded jeans to wear.

She continued to gaze out the window. The staff quarters were at the back of the lodge, so the view was mostly of snow-moving machines, which looked like weird prehistoric monsters under their coverings of snow, half-buried dumpsters, and the back side of the beginners' slope. But if Jill pressed her face up close to the glass, she could see a steep slope beyond the lodge and the black parallel lines of the lifts. The main slopes were still empty that early in the morning, and the lifts were not running yet, but as she watched, she saw a lone skier in a red jacket come flying down, shooting up a trail of silvery spray behind him. His descent looked so effortless and so exciting that Jill longed to try it for herself. She had never been a great skier, but now that she was older and more confident—maybe she would fly down the hillside like that skier.

Then her thoughts turned to Jake. She imagined how great he would look in a red ski jacket, his eyes shining and his hair blowing in the wind as he flew down the ski run. She pictured herself skiing beside him, managing to match his speed. At the bottom he would turn and scoop her up into his arms. "You're improving all the time," he would say. "I'm going to have to stay in shape to beat you." And his lips would feel warm in spite of the snow, and they would turn and walk toward his cabin together. . . .

Stop it, Jill said severely to herself. *You have to stop thinking about him. You are going to have a good time here with Toni, make some money, do a little skiing, and forget about men! Understand?*

Her thoughts were interrupted by an urgent whisper from down the hall. Jill poked her head around the door and saw Toni peering anxiously from the bathroom.

"Jill," she hissed, "I left in such a hurry that I forgot to bring my towel."

Jill smiled sweetly. "That will teach you to beat me to the bathroom," she said and pretended to turn away.

"Jill!" said Toni more urgently. "I don't have a towel in here. I'm dripping all over the floor."

"So what do you plan to do about it?" Jill asked. "You could always streak down the hall."

"Oh, come on," Toni pleaded. "Don't be so mean. Go get my towel for me, please."

"Only if you promise that you will never beat me to the bathroom again," Jill said, grinning.

"Okay, I promise. Now, hurry up, I'm freezing in here."

"And," Jill persisted, "that you will never again trick me into doing something I wouldn't want to do if I knew about it."

"Okay, I promise. I promise! Now *please* get my towel."

Jill laughed and walked down the hall with the towel in her hand. "Here," she said. "And just consider yourself lucky that I didn't make you promise any more than that."

Toni snatched the towel. "You are turning into a hard-hearted person, Jill Gardner," she muttered as she closed the door behind her.

They were on their way down to breakfast when they bumped into Mr. Swensen himself. "Hello, ladies," he said. "I hear you did a good job yesterday. In fact, you were so good that I decided I didn't even need to fix my dishwasher." He took one look at their horrified faces and laughed. "Relax. I was only joking. The repairman is coming to fix it today. Go see Maria and tell her I sent you to help her. She's the housekeeper, and she has to make this place look extra nice by this evening. We've got important guests coming. I want us to look good, understand?"

"Yes, sir," the girls muttered and walked on, giving each other puzzled looks.

"I hope Maria is an improvement over Heavy Hilda," Toni said when Mr. Swensen was out of earshot.

"And I hope we're allowed to eat breakfast before we start," Jill added. "I'm starving. I didn't eat a thing yesterday. I got so bummed out by all those pots and pans that I couldn't stand the thought of food. But I feel like making up for it now."

"Me, too," Toni agreed. "The good thing is we can eat as much as we like up here and then ski off all the extra calories."

"If we ever get any time off," Jill reminded her friend. "You didn't ask Mr. Swensen about it, I notice."

Toni wrinkled her nose. "I didn't think it was the right time," she said. "It's hardly diplomatic to arrive at a place and immediately start asking about time off, is it?"

As they clomped down the back stairs to the staff cafeteria, a door opened and a distinguished-looking woman dressed in black came out.

"I'm sorry, this hallway only leads to the service area," she said to them. "You have to take that door on your right to get back into the lodge."

"We're going down to the staff cafeteria," Jill said uncertainly. "We work here."

The woman eyed them suspiciously, then suddenly looked as if she understood. "Oh, you must be the two girls who arrived yesterday. Mr. Swensen had you sent straight down to cope with the kitchen emergency, I understand. Not a very pleasant welcome to Snowfire, was it?"

"Let's say we both got a bad case of dishpan hands," Toni said, smiling back.

The woman held out her own hand to Toni. "I'm Maria. I'm the housekeeper here," she said. "And you are—?"

"Toni—and Jill."

"Pleased to meet you both. Are you going to be working in the kitchen again today?"

"Mr. Swensen told us to report to you," Jill said hurriedly. "He said you would need extra help today."

Maria smiled broadly. "That's good. I can sure use a few extra hands. Mr. Swensen's always fussy, but today, with the important guests coming . . . We need the copper hood on the fireplace polished, the slate floor polished, the mirror polished—everything polished, in fact. Follow me, and we'll get you a couple of uniforms."

"Actually," Toni said, "we were on our way to get some breakfast first; if that's okay with you."

"Of course," Maria said, nodding at them. "You both look as if you could use a square meal. Go and get a good breakfast, and then come up and look for me in the lobby. I'll show you where all the cleaning equipment is kept and what we have to do."

"She's *definitely* an improvement over Heavy Hilda," Toni commented as they walked into the cafeteria. "I don't think she'll yell and grunt at us."

"She seemed very nice," Jill said. "I wonder who these important guests are? How about if the president or Prince Charles and Lady Di are arriving tonight?"

"How about Bruce Springsteen or Tom Selleck?" Toni answered, grinning.

"Your trouble is, you don't have a romantic streak," Jill said, helping herself to a glass of orange juice and a plate of scrambled eggs.

Several other girls in maids' uniforms looked up with interest as they sat down. "Are you the new maids?" one asked.

"We're new, but I'm not sure what we are," Jill said. "Yesterday we were in the kitchen, today we have polishing duty."

A large blond girl looked at them suspiciously. "Better than making beds all day," she said. "You should see what your back feels like after making twenty-five beds."

"I didn't think they were hiring any more staff," the redhead beside her commented. "They told Aileen there were no more openings."

"Oh, we're just here for the vacation," Jill said and instantly regretted her remark.

"Oh, you're college girls?" the blond said,

giving her friends a meaningful look. "They're college girls, Trina, so watch your language."

"No wonder they get the easy jobs," the redhead commented.

Jill could feel Toni stirring beside her. "If you call washing filthy pots and pans for ten hours straight an easy job, you are even dumber than you look," she said. "We got out of that kitchen at eleven-thirty last night with a terminal case of dishpan hands. Let me tell you, that is no fun job."

"Okay, okay. Keep your shirt on," the blond said. "Like, we're just not used to college girls on the domestic staff. Most of them are out on the lifts or helping with the ski lessons, stuff like that."

"We're more the domestic type, aren't we, Jill?" Toni said.

Jill laughed. "That's not exactly the adjective I would use to describe you," she said with a smirk. "Remember that spaghetti you tried to cook?"

"If you tell them about that, you're a dead woman," Toni said hastily. "Let's change the subject, okay? I'm Toni, by the way, and this is my friend Jill."

"Marlene," the blond girl said. "That's Trina, and Joanie. I guess we'd better be getting to work. Mr. Swensen is going to inspect the rooms himself today, with all the V.I.P.s coming."

"Do you know exactly who's coming?" Jill asked. "We've got to polish everything."

"You mean you haven't heard about the

movie?" Marlene asked. "There are millions of rumors going around about which movie stars are going to be coming."

"They're going to shoot a movie here?" Jill asked incredulously.

"That's right," Trina said, her eyes shining. "They're going to be here for two whole weeks. Just think, we might bump into somebody famous in the hallway. I might have to make Robert Redford's bed!"

"We'd better get moving then," Marlene said, lifting her large body from the bench. "Or we'll all get fired before they arrive."

The three girls filed out, leaving Jill and Toni alone. Toni kept shoveling scrambled eggs and bacon into her mouth. Jill eyed her suspiciously. "Did you know they were going to shoot a movie here?" she asked coldly.

"How would I know that?" Toni said. "I only found out when you did."

"It just seems like a pretty big coincidence, knowing you," Jill said.

"Knowing *what* about me?" Toni demanded.

"That you want to break into show biz. You planned to get a job here and then be discovered as you were polishing the fireplace, right?"

"Wrong," Toni said. "The thought never crossed my mind."

"Toni Redmond," Jill said sternly, "do you solemnly swear that you did not come here with the idea of getting a part in this movie?"

"I solemnly swear," Toni said in a hurt voice. "Now are you satisfied?"

"I guess I'll have to be," Jill said. "But I still think there's something you're not telling me."

"Like what?" Toni asked, pushing away her empty plate.

"I plan to find out," Jill said.

ELEVEN

The finishing touches still were not completed when the first people from the movie company walked in. Jill was staggering toward the front door, carrying an enormous Christmas wreath to hang there, when a van pulled up and several young people climbed out. They were all dressed very casually in jeans and down jackets. The girls didn't look as if they were wearing any makeup, and some of the men had hair almost as long as the girls'. Before a bellboy could arrive, they started unloading stuff from the van.

Hotel staff rushed to the scene immediately, and the bellboy bent down to pick up some of the steel cases.

"Uh, no thanks, just leave that stuff," a man with a beard said pleasantly. "We'd rather bring it in ourselves. These cameras cost a fortune. But you can take our personal bags if you want." And he indicated a growing pile of duffel bags and backpacks.

Jill finished hanging up her wreath and went back inside.

"Is that them?" Marlene asked her excitedly after Jill had reported back to the housekeeper. "Do they look real glamorous? I gotta go take a peek. Did you see any stars?"

Jill laughed. "They are about as unglamorous as you can get," she said. "They look like refugees from a camping trip, but I guess they're just the crew. The stars will probably make a grand entrance later." But Marlene was still excited and scurried away to take a look.

"Did you hear that the movie people have started to arrive already?" Jill asked Toni, who was stocking the fireplace with logs and showing an uncharacteristic lack of interest.

"Oh, really?" Toni said. "Did Tom Selleck walk in yet?"

"Nobody famous walked in," Jill said. "Marlene is going to be disappointed. She thinks all movie people arrive wearing mink coats and sunglasses. Instead they look more like college students. Oh, look," Jill said, crossing to a window, "there's another load of them arriving now. That must be the director, don't you think?" she asked as Toni joined her. He's already looking around to see what camera angles to use—" She broke off suddenly and grabbed Toni's arm. "Toni," she hissed.

"Doesn't that guy look like Brandt? The one in the parka?"

"Oh, my god!" Toni exclaimed. "It *is* Brandt. Quick, Jill. In here. Don't let him see me." She clutched at Jill and dragged her through a door to the service hall.

"Toni, what's the matter with you?" Jill asked, eyeing her friend suspiciously.

"Boy, what a surprise, to see Brandt here. I had no idea—" Toni said.

"And he doesn't know you're working here?" Jill asked. "He's going to be surprised, too. What were you running away for? You two are still going together, aren't you?"

"Oh, sure," Toni said.

"So he's going to be so happy to find out you're here!"

"I hope so," Toni said.

"So go out and surprise him!" Jill insisted. "I can't wait to see his face when he sees you."

"Uh, not now," Toni said. "I mean, not in this gross uniform. It's two sizes too big for me, I never did look good in brown, and I look like a refugee from an orphanage. Take a look, Jill, and tell me if he's still there."

Jill poked her head around the door. "He's still there," she said.

"Then let's find something to do in the kitchen for a while," Toni said, dragging Jill.

"I can't understand why you don't want him to see you," Jill said. "I mean, what could be nicer than finding that your girlfriend is in the same place as you? He'll be so happy—"

"I hope so," Toni said again.

"Why shouldn't he be?" Jill demanded.

"No reason," Toni said airily. "I'll let him discover I'm here when I'm looking a little more glamorous. I've got to compete with all those starlets, you know."

She hurried down the hall ahead of Jill and started unloading the dishwasher, banging mugs on the shelf as she put them down. Jill stared at her with a puzzled expression.

"Toni?" she ventured at last. "Did Brandt happen to mention to you that he might be filming at a ski resort?"

"He might have," Toni said, still banging the mugs but not looking up.

Jill sighed. "I think this whole thing is beginning to make sense," she said.

"What do you mean?" Toni asked sharply.

"I mean, why you suddenly came up with this wonderful job for vacation," Jill said, staring hard at Toni.

"It *is* a great job," Toni said defensively. "And it's pure coincidence that Brandt happened to choose this place."

"I'll bet it is," Jill said with a grim smile. "Why don't you ever tell the truth, Toni? At least to me— I'm supposed to be your best friend, remember."

"Are you trying to say that I lied to you?" Toni turned and gave Jill her hurt-little-girl look.

Jill nodded. "I'm trying to say that you knew Brandt was going to be working at this ski resort. Then you persuaded the manager to give you a job here. Am I right?"

"I guess so," Toni growled, looking down at her feet.

"And you tricked me into coming here, Toni," Jill said angrily. "That's what really hurts—that you didn't trust your best friend enough to tell her the real reason you wanted to come here so desperately."

Toni continued to stare at the toes of her sneakers. "I'm really sorry, Jill," she said. "I know it must look like that to you, but I didn't want to trick you. Honestly I didn't. You see, the person I was really deceiving was me. I fed myself all these good arguments for taking a job here, and I almost convinced myself that wanting to work here had nothing to do with Brandt. Until I saw him, that is. Then I suddenly realized what I'd done."

"But why, Toni?" Jill asked, giving her friend an understanding look. "What made you so desperate all of a sudden? Everything's going well between you and Brandt, isn't it?"

Toni sighed. "I suddenly got scared, Jill, when he decided to work on this movie. I thought he'd be meeting all these movie stars and he'd forget about me. I just wanted to keep an eye on him. Dumb idea, huh?"

"About average for you," Jill said, managing a smile. "But what I don't understand is why you don't rush out and throw your arms around him, now that you've got him here. Isn't that what you wanted?"

"It was," Toni said. "But now I just feel stupid. As soon as I saw him I knew I'd done the wrong thing. He'll think I'm spying on him, and he'll be mad at me, Jill. He won't ever want to talk to me again. I've got to be sure he doesn't see me."

Jill shook her head. "I used to think you were a little crazy, but now I know you're *really* crazy. Why are you so sure he'll be mad at you? If I found that the person I liked best in the world was staying at the same place I was, I'd be overjoyed. I'd take it as a compliment that that person wanted to be near me. Why don't you go out and give it a try?"

"I can't." Toni sighed. "We had such a good relationship, Jill. I just can't risk blowing it."

Jill helped her unload a large spaghetti pot and put it on its hook. "Well," she said, "I don't really see how you can keep hiding from him for three weeks. This place isn't that large, you know. Someday someone's going to send you to clean up the tables, and he's going to be sitting at one."

"Don't," Toni begged. "I can't bear to think about it. Why don't we both quit and go home right now?"

"But I'm just beginning to like it here," Jill said. "The rest of the staff is friendly, the work's not too hard, and I met this guy at lunch who operates the triple chair lift, and promised to help me with my skiing. I don't want to go home."

"If you really cared about me as a friend—" Toni began, but Jill interrupted her. "Now, don't go into your little-girl act with me, Toni Redmond. You've done all the manipulating you're going to do. You got me up here because you had a secret reason for wanting to be here. I came because I didn't want to let my best friend down. But now that I'm here, I'm going to stay. You can leave if you want to—that's fine with me. I'll just get your quilt plus mine to keep me warm at night. Now I'm going back to get those logs you didn't bring in," she said firmly. Then she turned and walked out of the kitchen, leaving an abashed Toni staring after her.

TWELVE

"What's he doing now?" Toni demanded. Jill opened the service door a fraction of an inch and peeped through. "He's still sitting and talking with that group of people over by the fire," she said.

Toni grunted. "Why can't he go out and start filming? No wonder they charge five dollars to see movies these days. All the time they waste before they even start shooting."

Jill shook her head, smiling. "Toni, they have to plan their shooting for the day, and they can't do that outside when the temperature is minus something with the wind-chill factor." She turned to her friend and touched her arm. "It's never going to work, you know. You can't keep avoiding him for two weeks. Sooner or later you're bound to run into each other, and then he'll think you were crazy to hide from him."

"We won't run into each other if I keep doing all

the jobs down in the kitchen and you do all the jobs out in the guest area," she said.

"But, Toni!" Jill said fiercely. "What are you accomplishing by hiding from him?"

"He won't know I'm a jealous, suspicious, and untrusting person. And he won't decide he never wants to see me again, that's what."

"But you'll never pull it off, Toni," Jill said in a kindly way. "Someday it's bound to come out. Someday you'll forget and say something about Snowfire and he'll find out. Or you might even get married and mumble the word 'Snowfire' in your sleep. I wish you'd go out there, act pleasantly surprised, and let life go on again. Living with you is like living with the CIA. I can't keep on peering around corners and hiding in closets. It's making me a nervous wreck."

Toni twisted her hair around her finger, something she always did when she was under extreme stress. "I'll think about it, Jill. I'll see if I can get up enough courage, but not right now. So please, *please*, be an angel and go wash those tables for me and let me polish the floor back here for you."

"Well, I guess so," Jill said. "Only what happens when I meet him? He'll remember me and ask about you, and you know how I hate to lie."

"He probably won't notice you," Toni said bitterly. "There are several great-looking girls sitting right beside him."

"You sure know how to flatter a person," Jill said, half amused.

Toni grinned. "I didn't mean that you're not gorgeous," she said. "It's just that people don't usually notice what maids and waitresses look like, especially when they are surrounded by distractions like that girl on his left, who must have been poured into that pink angora sweater. Especially since we all look like oversized Tootsie Rolls in these horrible brown uniforms."

"So if nobody notices waitresses, why don't you get out there yourself?"

"I don't trust myself," Toni said angrily. "I might be tempted to pour cold coffee all over the pink angora sweater. So let me do the polishing for you, okay? You want this hall done first?"

Toni's voice rose over the noise of the polisher as she turned it on.

"Hey, wait a minute," Jill shouted. "You'd better let me show you. That machine is a big industrial model, and it's not that easy—" But she was never able to finish the sentence, because Toni shot off down the hall, dragged along by the twirling wheels of the polisher. "How do you control this thing?" she yelled. "Help, it's running away with me! Jill—do something!"

But before Jill could do anything, the polisher went crashing out through the swinging doors and into the main lobby. Toni's screams mingled with startled yells and shouts and the occasional crash of something falling. Jill ran after Toni only to see her shoot across the slate floor, wrestling desperately with a handle which jerked with a life of its own, bounce off a couple of surprised skiers, knock over some luggage, and finally bump into a sofa before the polisher fell onto its side and lay there, pads whirring helplessly, like a giant wounded insect. Jill rushed out to turn off the motor, but one of Brandt's group got there first. The man with the beard calmly flipped the switch, and there was sudden silence.

"I'm really very sorry," gasped Toni, "I had no idea it was so strong and had a mind of its own."

"That's okay," the bearded man said, giving her a kindly smile. "No harm done apart from scaring us all out of our minds. We were just discussing a scene where this horrible snow monster leaps up and grabs a competitor in the slalom race, when all of a sudden *this* monster machine comes crashing into us. I'd better check whether any of my crew has died of heart failure. Anyone dead here?"

Everyone was laughing except Brandt. He had risen to his feet. "Toni—what on earth are you doing here?" he stammered.

"Hi, Brandt. Surprise!" Toni mumbled.

Brandt started smiling. "I might have known when I saw a machine flying along out of control that nobody else could have been involved." He took her hands. "You little nut," he said. "Are you sure you're all right?"

Toni nodded. Brandt went on looking at her. "But what are you doing here?" he asked. "I thought I was hallucinating when I looked up and saw you."

"That's me," Toni mumbled. "Just a hallucination. You can go back to your work now, and I'll evaporate into the nothingness from which I came."

"But you're all shaken up," Brandt said. "Let's go and have a cup of coffee and relax, and you can tell me about this incredible coincidence."

Jill watched with mixed feelings as Toni and Brandt walked through the room toward the snack bar. Brandt had his hand resting easily on her shoulder. Toni lifted her face to look at him, and Jill could see that it already had that special glowing look that sometimes shone from Toni when she was very happy.

"I only hope it stays that way," Jill muttered to herself. "I only hope that he's still pleased to see her when he finds out that she sneaked up here to keep an eye on him."

The two figures passed through the doorway and out of sight. For a second she wondered if she should go and help Toni explain. Toni was not very good at explaining. For some reason she would rather tell the most unbelievable story than tell the truth. At this moment she was probably telling Brandt that she had been kidnapped and brought up to the lodge as a slave, or that she had decided to join the international ski circuit.

Well, it's up to her, Jill thought, struggling to right the heavy machine. *It's her life, and she's got to live it however she wants to.* She was just dragging the polisher back toward the service area when Mr. Swensen emerged from his office.

"Oh, no," he said to her in a shocked whisper.

"We do not polish the guest areas at this time of day. We don't want to upset people with the noise. Get that thing back where it belongs at once." Jill opened her mouth to say something but couldn't find any words that didn't involve casting blame on Toni. Mr. Swensen looked around critically. "And those coffee tables," he said. "They should have been cleared off long ago. We can't let dirty glasses accumulate like that. See to that first, will you." He shook his head. "Your friend convinced me that you were both very experienced in the hospitality industry. I expected better than this from you." Then he stalked away, leaving Jill with tears stinging her eyes.

After that she worked feverishly, not wanting Mr. Swensen to demand, "Shouldn't there be two people working this area?"

It was really hard work to control the giant polisher, and Jill was just dragging it down the hall toward the closet when Toni appeared again.

"Nice timing," Jill said, pausing to push her hair out of her eyes. "I hope my slave labor was worth it."

"You're wonderful," Toni said, beaming at her. "You're a terrific friend, and I'm going to remember you in my will."

"Don't tell me—you're going to hire me as a grave digger," Jill said dryly. "So I take it from that silly grin on your face that you explained everything satisfactorily to Brandt, and he is delighted to see you again?"

Toni nodded. "It all went beautifully, Jill. I just told him the truth about how much I missed him when he went away, and then I saw this job advertised and it seemed like too big a coincidence, so I decided it must be fate—"

"Wait a minute," Jill interrupted. "You did not see this job advertised. You called Mr. Swensen on the phone and begged him to hire you!"

Toni wrinkled her nose. "So I mostly told the truth—who cares about a few details?"

"You are hopeless, Toni Redmond," Jill said, smiling. "But I gather that Brandt was not mad at you for following him?"

"Not at all," Toni said. "He said he missed me a lot, too, and had toyed with the idea of calling me and asking me to join him. Wasn't that sweet?"

"I'm very glad for you," Jill said. "And I'm very thankful that I don't have to spend the rest of my time here peering around corners and crossing rooms disguised as a table lamp. Also, you'll be able to do your share of the work again!"

Toni grinned. "Sorry about that," she said. "But I had to go and straighten things out while I still had the courage."

"Of course you did. And I don't mind doing favors for you once in a while—as long as you don't start taking them for granted."

"Of course not," Toni said. "But while you're in such a nice mood, I have one more teeny-weeny favor to ask. Brandt wants to have lunch with me—"

"But, Toni—you know what chaos the outside lunch line is! We need you out there."

"Just this once, Jill—please," Toni begged. "After today he's going to be out shooting all the time, and I'll hardly get to see him at all. Please, cover for me today. I'll make it up to you, I promise. Someday when you have a special guy and you want time to be alone with him, I'll do all your work, and go to your lectures for you, and even write your papers—"

"Not my papers," Jill said firmly. "I want to graduate from college one of these days. But I suppose I can handle the hamburgers without you—just this once."

Toni flung her arms around Jill. "I won't ever forget this," she said. "I'll spend the rest of my life telling the world what a wonderful person you are."

Then she danced off down the hall, leaving Jill to drag the polisher the rest of the way to the utility closet.

THIRTEEN

Jill looked at her watch. It was almost midnight. She had not gone off duty until after eight, then had eaten a lonely supper down in the employees' cafeteria while Toni was dining in style with Brandt in the fancy restaurant upstairs.

"I'm glad you're here to keep an eye on Toni," Brandt had said when he came to pick Toni up. "Although, if I were you, I'd keep her away from floor polishers in the future. She can be incredibly dangerous without even trying." And he had gazed down fondly at Toni while she tried to fix him with one of her withering stares. "I hope you don't mind if I steal her for the evening," he had said to Jill. "But once filming starts I'm going to be running around like crazy. The title 'assistant director' simply means doing everything nobody else wants to do."

Jill had smiled and said that of course she didn't mind, then she watched them walk away, holding hands like little kids. She tried not to feel bad, telling herself that she was really glad that everything had worked out for Toni and Brandt, but her dinner seemed extra tasteless, the surroundings extra bleak, and the chatter coming from Marlene and the other maids extra stupid. She only toyed with her chili before making an excuse to get away from their animated discussion about movie stars.

A group of kids who worked on the ski slopes came in and sat down far from Jill's group. Jill looked longingly at their sun-tanned faces. She would have liked to have joined them, but in the lodge there was clearly a division between the domestic staff and the ski slope workers. But when she heard them discussing a new racing binding, she knew she would have felt like an outsider there, too.

There was a big TV screen at the other end of the cafeteria and a few vinyl-covered chairs, which were about as inviting to sit on as an icy sidewalk, but Jill pretended to be interested in the program, rather than having to talk to the other kids. After they left she hung around watching TV until her whole body ached. When she finally went to face the icy chill of her room, she found that Toni had not returned.

She's going to be sorry in the morning that she stayed up so late, Jill thought, climbing into her bed and pulling the covers up over her head. *I bet she'll be a real grouch when I try to wake her for breakfast tomorrow.*

The room felt extra cold that night, and Jill curled into a tight ball, trying to get warm. Her feet were like two lumps of ice, no matter what she did to warm them. Finally, after she had gotten up and put on her ski socks, she drifted off into a restless sleep.

She woke to find that her quilt had slipped off onto the floor and that her back was as cold as if she had snuggled up against a snowdrift. "Just after I managed to get to sleep, too," she muttered, reaching down for the quilt and throwing it back over herself. She glanced at Toni's bed. It was still empty. *How could she stay out this late?* Jill thought angrily. *It must be way after midnight by now.* Out of habit she reached for her little alarm clock with the luminous dial. She glanced at it, then put it up to her ear to see if it was still working. The clock did not say midnight at all. It said six-thirty.

Jill sat there staring at the clock, feeling the icy draft from the window. She felt strangely sick and empty inside. She got up and peered out the window. Sure enough, there was a faint gray streak of morning at the top of the hill. Jill climbed back into bed and lay there, shivering and staring at the ceiling until the blue snowy light gradually lit the room. Then she got up and dressed mechanically.

She was just brushing her hair when Toni walked in.

"Hi," Toni said casually as she started to take a clean uniform out of the closet.

Jill went on brushing her hair. "Next time you might warn me in advance if you're not coming back all night," she said, still not taking her eyes off her reflection in the mirror. "I sure could have used your quilt."

"I didn't exactly plan it in advance," Toni said, banging the closet door shut.

"Look, Toni—" Jill began, but Toni cut her off. "I don't want to talk right now, okay? I've got to get down to help with breakfast." She grabbed her uniform and headed for the bathroom, leaving Jill feeling even more sick and confused.

Toni hardly said a word all through breakfast, working swiftly and mechanically putting sausages and strips of bacon onto plates. The moment the meal was served she hurried out to her next chore. Jill felt as if she had been slapped in the face. There had never been a time in their whole friendship when Toni had shut her out like this. In the past, Toni had yelled and screamed and then refused to talk to her for a few days—but never this cold, polite silence, as if Jill were a stranger. Jill tried to force down a slice of toast, but her throat refused to swallow. Was this really the end of their closeness, forever? Or did Toni just need to be by herself for a little while right then? Jill wished she were a little older and wiser. *If only I hadn't acted so cold toward Toni when she first walked in,* she thought miserably. *But I was confused and upset. I guess I'm not used to the fact that we're all grown-up now. We can make our own decisions, and there's nobody around to tell us what to do and what not to do. But it's all so hard. I'd love to go back in time to when we used to go out on dates and kiss good night on the front porch and then go in to our moms and dads. Everything was so much simpler then.*

She went into the bathroom and took off the cap

she had to wear while serving meals. *What's wrong with me?* she demanded, staring at herself critically in the mirror. *Why do things upset me that don't seem to upset anybody else? So Toni and Brandt chose to spend the night together. That's not such a big deal, is it? After all, they've known each other for a couple of months. She lives in her own apartment. Nobody's there to check on what she does. I have to find some way to tell her that it's okay, that whatever she does is all right with me.*

But it seemed as if Jill was not going to get the chance to talk to Toni. All morning Toni worked feverishly, rushing from one chore to the next. She went down to lunch ahead of Jill and gulped down the last of her hamburger as Jill came in the door. In the afternoon they both were sent to wash windows. Again Toni chose to occupy herself as far away from Jill as possible, working with an intensity Jill had never seen her demonstrate. Jill sighed and looked back at her pail of soapy water. What fun things like washing windows used to be. She could imagine doing something like this a few years ago: Toni slopping water everywhere or getting a drop in her eye and screaming out that she was blinded, probably kicking over the pail as she danced around. But now she was like an efficient robot, dipping her squeegee into the water and reaching her arm up like a mechanical crane.

Mr. Swensen came by around midafternoon. "Now, that's more like it," he said warmly. "You're both as busy as two little bees. That's how I like to see my workers perform. Keep at it."

How wrong can you be? Jill thought bitterly. Mr. Swensen obviously knew nothing about life at all, or he would be able to see two people who were working hard in order to avoid talking to each other. And it wasn't that Jill didn't try.

"Here," she said to Toni once. "Take this rag, yours is already dirty."

"Thanks," Toni said, taking the rag and moving back to her old position.

Jill was about to launch into a conversation when Toni threw down her rag and sprinted across the room. "Oh, there's Brandt," she called. Jill watched as Toni danced outside and across the snow toward him, and he caught her up in his arms and twirled her around like a little kid. Mechanically she picked up Toni's bucket as well as her own and took them back to the kitchen.

"Has anyone cleared off the tables yet?" Maria demanded, looking down at several of the employees who were sitting around drinking coffee or smoking cigarettes.

"I'm on my first break all day," someone mumbled. "We only sat down."

Maria turned around and saw Jill. "Would you just run up and clear off the tables, honey?" she asked pleasantly. "These girls have been sorting laundry, and they need a few minutes' rest. You don't mind, do you?"

"No, I don't mind," Jill said, trying not to look as grouchy as she felt. Actually, she did mind a lot. The last place in the world she wanted to be right then was in the lounge. Toni would probably be there with Brandt.

She asked herself why it made her so angry to see them together as she went back upstairs to the lounge. Could it be that she was jealous? Of course that was part of the answer. She knew only too well that she could have been with Jake at that very moment, walking with his arm around her the way Toni had walked with Brandt. She had only come to this lodge because of Toni, and now Toni was making it very clear that she didn't want her around anymore. Somehow it didn't seem fair.

But you're the one who decided to come, she argued with herself. *You didn't want to find yourself in a difficult situation with Jake. You knew what might happen if you were alone with him in an isolated cabin.*

As these thoughts raced through her brain, a clear picture of Jake filled her mind. He was smiling at her across the room, leaning against the wall and looking relaxed, his eyes sparkling. Jill felt a strange twisting in her stomach. Would Jake ever look at her like that again? She knew that Jake was not the sort of person who would wait around all vacation for a girl. What if he greeted her politely when they met again after winter break, but didn't look at her in that special way anymore? Suddenly the thought of life at Rosemont without Jake seemed very bleak and depressing.

"If only—" she found herself murmuring as she pushed open the swinging doors to the lounge. A quick glance around the room showed her that Toni and Brandt were not there, but that was of little comfort to her. Everyone else in the room seemed to be part of a couple, sitting cozily together with firelight reflected on their faces. It was as if the whole world had suddenly paired off, leaving Jill as the only single one. Hurriedly Jill stacked empty cups and plates onto her tray. All she wanted to do was clear off the low tables and get out of there fast. She had no desire to hang around, watching everyone else looking so happy.

When the tray was piled as high as possible, she lifted it and made for the door.

"Hey, miss," a voice called from a dark corner beside the fire. "You left some glasses over here."

"I'll be back in a minute," Jill said, not too politely. "I can only carry so many at one time, you know. I can't perform miracles."

"Can't you?" asked the voice. For the first time Jill focused on the person who was talking.

"Jake?" she asked in a quavering voice. He was sitting just out of range of the firelight at a corner table, wearing an oversized turtleneck sweater. Relaxed as usual, he was leaning back in his chair and watching her. Jill put down the tray before she dropped it.

"In the flesh," Jake said, his eyes laughing at her. "You're looking at me as though I were a ghost."

"But I was just—" Jill muttered. For a moment she really had wondered whether she had been having an hallucination. "What are you doing here?" she asked. "I thought you were at your cabin at Lake Tahoe."

"The cabin was boring," Jake said. "I got snowed in with my brother and his girlfriend. They had a fight on the first day and weren't speaking to each other. So we played endless stupid games— would you believe that I now know the answer to every question of Trivial Pursuit? Go on, test me. Ask the capital of Afghanistan and the number of home runs Babe Ruth hit."

"Jake," Jill said, shaking her head and laughing at the same time. "I can't believe that you're here."

Jake rose from his chair, came around the table, and kissed her. "Now do you believe it?" he asked her. "You told me the only way I could go skiing with you was to come up to Snowfire, so here I am."

"You mean you've come up here to stay?" she stammered. "How did you get a room?"

"They had a single cancellation. And I'll stay as long as you want me," he said softly.

Suddenly Jill remembered that she was standing in the middle of the lounge, wearing her brown-and-white uniform, kissing one of the customers. Somehow she had a feeling that Mr. Swensen might not approve of that. She pushed Jake away from her.

"Look, I'm still on duty," she said, feeling her cheeks becoming almost as hot as the fire. "I've got to clear off these tables, but I'll see if I can get off after that."

"I'll be waiting," Jake said.

As she walked through the swinging doors, she glanced back and saw him still watching her.

FOURTEEN

When Jill returned to the kitchen, staggering under the weight of the laden tray, she found that the only other person there was Toni, busily unloading glasses from the dishwasher.

"Hi," Jill said.

Toni turned around uneasily. "Hi," she answered and went back to unloading glasses.

"What happened to Brandt?" Jill asked. "I thought you'd be having dinner with him again."

"He had to go to a planning session in the director's room," Toni said in a flat voice. "He expects it to go on all evening."

"Oh," Jill said. "Well, in that case, do you mind if I ask you something?"

"Look, Jill, I don't want a lecture from you!" Toni said sharply.

Jill looked hurt and surprised. "I wasn't going

to give you a lecture," she said. "What made you think that?"

"The way you looked at me this morning," Toni said. "When I came back into the room, you gave me a look that said you were about to tell me what your great-aunt Mabel had told you!"

Jill started to smile. "You're an idiot," she said. "I would never do that."

"But that was how you looked," Toni protested. "Like the queen of England peering at a cockroach."

"Come on, Toni," Jill said. "I admit that I felt kind of angry and confused, partly because I hadn't slept too well. I guess I felt kind of like a mother whose kid is about to dart out under a car—scared and angry, too, that the kid had made her feel scared."

Toni looked up at Jill. "You don't have to feel scared for me, Jill," she said. "Everything's just fine—and I'm a big girl now."

"I know that, Toni," Jill said. "I think Brandt's a great person, and I only have to take one look at the two of you together to tell how you feel about each other. It's just that I'm sort of slow at learning to cope with new experiences. You know how hard it was for me to adjust to having a college roommate. . . ."

"Nobody could have adjusted to Sheridan," Toni said. "I bet even her mother couldn't wait to get rid of her. But I'm really glad you don't mind about Brandt and me because he means everything in the world to me, Jill, and I'd hate to have to choose between you and him."

"You'll never have to do that," Jill said. "We promised not to interfere in each others' lives, didn't we? Besides, it's a new experience to watch you stay in love with the same guy for three months. I'm thinking of entering it into the *Guinness Book of World Records*."

"Oh, shut up," Toni said. "I never teased you about Craig or Carlo."

"Yes, you did," Jill said. "Mercilessly."

"Oh, well, I promise not to tease you next time," Toni said. "When you get all dreamy eyed over Jake or somebody."

"Speaking of Jake," Jill said, noticing that her voice trembled when she said his name. "What I was going to ask you was a favor."

"Ask away," Toni said.

"Since Brandt's going to be busy all evening, I wondered if you'd take my late duty for me. It just so happens that Jake has arrived, and—"

"Jake? Arrived here?" Toni yelled. Her voice echoed through the cavernous kitchen.

"Shh! Don't tell the whole world," Jill said. "He got here this afternoon."

"But I thought he was going to a cabin somewhere," Toni said, eyeing Jill's flaming cheeks with interest.

"He was," Jill said. "But he said it was too boring, so he came here instead."

"For how long?" Toni asked.

"For as long as I want him to stay," Jill stammered, blushing even more deeply.

Toni beamed. "Wow, Jill, that's terrific," she said. "He really must care about you if he's chasing you like this—and paying the price of the rooms here! Do you know what they're charging? It would be cheaper to buy a plot of land and build your own cabin, I swear."

"Ah, but the guests' rooms have lots of heat," Jill said. "Last night I think I would have paid anything to be warm."

Toni's face clouded over. "I'm sorry I kept you awake and got you worried," she said. "But I'm going to make it up to you now. I'll take over all your work so you and Jake can spend as much time as you want together—starting tonight. You get out of here right now and go put on your sexiest dress."

"Thanks, Toni," Jill said. She turned toward the door, then looked back. "On second thought, maybe not my sexiest dress," she said. "That guy doesn't need any encouragement!"

Toni's giggles followed her down the hall.

Back in their room Jill eyed her wardrobe critically. She had brought up her best clothes because Toni had promised that they'd be going to lots of parties. Her hands passed over the slinky black dress with the rhinestone straps and the very low-cut back. *It's true*, she thought with a smile. *That guy definitely does not need any encouragement*.

She paused, staring thoughtfully at the dress, fully realizing for the first time what had happened.

Jake was there, just as she had dreamed. Until that moment she had basked in the knowledge that he had come up to Snowfire to be with her. Now, suddenly, she realized the implications of their being alone together. He hadn't come all that way for nothing, after all. He was going to expect some commitment from her. Jill's hand trembled as she let the black fabric fall back into the closet. *I don't even know what I feel about him yet*, she thought as a small knot of fear began to grow in her stomach. *And I know I'm not ready for a closer relationship. What am I going to do? Toni's not going to be any help. She'll just tell me to do whatever feels right*. She picked up a fluffy white angora dress decorated with scattered pearls. It had a high cowl neck and long sleeves. Much more suitable, Jill decided. She took it out of the closet. *I guess I'll just have to play it by ear*, she thought as she started to change her clothes.

When she met him a half hour later, she saw that Jake had also changed. He was wearing a sort of Mexican peasant shirt that made him look like a character out of an old movie—the type of hero who swung down from balconies to rescue the pretty girl from bandits. He studied Jill approvingly. "That's much better," he said. "That uniform you were wearing was about the ugliest garment I have ever seen. It made you look like a nun in a polyester habit that had shrunk! Do you suppose they deliberately dress their staff like that so that the guests never take a second look at them?"

Jill laughed. "I must say, that is one of the most flattering opening lines ever spoken to me!"

"Oh, I didn't mean that you looked any less terrific," Jake said hastily. "You know your inner beauty always shines through. It's just that your outer beauty is seriously suppressed when you're dressed in something that makes you look like a cross between a prison warden and an orphan."

"Well, I'm glad my uniform is not like the costumes the cocktail waitresses have to wear here," Jill said. "You wait until you see them—tuxedo jackets and fishnet tights. That's all."

Jake eyed her appraisingly. "I bet you'd look good in a tux and fishnet tights."

"Maybe," Jill said, blushing slightly. "But I wouldn't want to be ogled as I did my work. At least now when I'm washing windows nobody even notices I'm around."

"You're right," Jake said. "I wouldn't want any other guys ogling you, either. Let's go get some dinner, okay? You're the expert—you'd better recommend what's good here." He slipped his arm around Jill's shoulder.

"There's no point in asking me," she said, "because the only time I've seen the dining room is when I've had to bring up clean silverware from the kitchen. We humble servants have to eat in the staff cafeteria where the menu doesn't get any more exotic than hot dogs or chili."

"In that case we'd better splurge in a big way

tonight," Jake said. "I feel like a good meal, too, after eating nothing but spaghetti and frozen dinners in the cabin."

"Don't expect any sympathy from me," Jill said, her eyes teasing him. "You haven't eaten the food in the staff cafeteria."

The hostess seated them at a small candlelit table by the window, giving Jill a quizzical glance as if she were wondering why someone who had been cleaning the windows earlier was now eating with such a good-looking guest. Jill pretended she didn't notice. She smiled at Jake in the candlelight. "So, there were just the three of you up at the cabin?"

Jake gave a heavy sigh. "Yes, and it couldn't have been worse. The very first evening they had a big fight, and they wouldn't speak to each other. I had to sit between them at the table while she said, 'Would you ask that gentleman down there to stop hogging the salt.' And then he said, 'Would you kindly tell that lady not to be so impatient, and that she can have the salt as soon as I'm finished with it.' Not a pleasant time, for sure. I spent the whole day on the slopes, well away from them. And I was planning to eat down at the lodge every evening, but then we had this big storm and we were snowed in for two days. In fact, I can't believe we've only been out of college a week. It seems like ten years. I spent the whole time thinking about you and how wonderful it would have been if you'd been there with me. The moment the snowplow reached our front door, I took off and came right up here. If we get snowbound now, I won't even care."

He reached across the table and took her hand. Jill felt the warmth of his fingers traveling all the way up her arm. "Are you pleased that I came?" he asked her in a low voice.

Jill wanted to tease him by saying, "Of course not. I was going to work my way through all the cute ski instructors, and now you've cramped my style." She tried to form the sentence in her head, but it was no use. She just couldn't be flippant. Instead she looked at him with shining eyes, and nodded.

"It's going to be so great," he said. "For the first time we're actually going to be alone with no roommates to bug us and no schoolwork waiting to be finished and no exams and no newspaper and no copy shop. Just you and me and all the time in the world."

The way he looked at her brought back the uneasiness she had felt alone in her room. "I do have work to do, Jake," she said. "Remember I'm up here because I have a job, so you'll have to be patient when I'm on duty."

"But you don't have to work in the evenings, do you?" he asked.

"Sometimes" she said. "I'm supposed to be on the day shift, and I get off around six."

"That's fine, then," he said. "I can keep myself busy skiing all day, helping all those cute little ski bunnies who have fallen down on the beginner slopes. Maybe even find somewhere quiet and write some poetry, which I haven't had time for in weeks. I'll find plenty to do. But you do get days off sometimes, don't you?"

"I've got two coming up," Jill said. "I worked a couple of extra-long shifts, so I can take two days off in a row."

"That's great," Jake said. "So tomorrow you can give me the grand tour of Snowfire, right?"

Jill laughed. "I'm afraid my grand tour would be limited to the kitchen, the linen closet, the housekeeper's room, and the broom closet."

"I don't suppose a cozy half hour in the linen closet would be so bad," Jake said, grinning at her. "Linen closets are usually warm, aren't they?"

"They also have a constant stream of maids coming in and out," Jill said severely. "Plus a housekeeper who sits there most of the time to check out the linen."

"So who needs a linen closet?" Jake asked. "Now, what do you want to eat? Should we really splurge and have lobster, or does the prime rib sound better?"

They lingered over dinner, talking and laughing easily. He was such good company that Jill relaxed completely and forgot any uneasiness she had felt. *I'm worrying for no reason*, she told herself. *He's a terrific person, and I'm so lucky he's here with me*.

"That was what I call a good meal," Jake said, leaning back contentedly in his chair. "Of course, maybe I'm only judging it against warmed-up spaghetti and TV dinners. What did you think?"

"Wonderful," Jill said. "I've never had crepes suzette before—I've only read about them. How exciting to have something actually set on fire at your table."

"I thought for a minute the waiter had poured on too much brandy," Jake said. "When the first flame shot up, it almost got his mustache."

Jill giggled. "I wondered why he had a reddish mustache when the rest of his hair was dark. Maybe it catches on fire a couple of times a week."

Jake took Jill's hand and helped her to her feet. "Now," he said, as they walked from the restaurant together, "I'm dying to see what your room looks like. Are you going to show me?"

Jill stiffened. "My room?" she asked. "You wouldn't want to see my room. It's like a prison cell and freezing cold. Even worse than a dorm room at Rosemont."

"That's terrible," Jake said. "I had no idea they treated their staff so badly. I'll complain to the manager in the morning and tell him that people can't work well when they are kept in subhuman conditions. Luckily they don't treat their guests the same way. My room is very cozy. Have you seen the third floor yet? It's got a sloping ceiling and built-in closets made of pine."

"You're lucky," Jill said. "Our furniture is strictly early Goodwill."

"So let's give your room a miss," Jake said, steering her along the hall. "Come on down to the desk and I'll get my key."

From down the hall came a burst of music. Jill grabbed Jake's arm. "But you haven't seen the disco yet," she said. "I've been dying to go in there, but I haven't had anyone to take me. We hear this great music when we've been down in the kitchen like Cinderellas. Let's go dance awhile, okay?"

"If you want to," Jake said. "Although I hope it's not too wild in there. I'm getting old, you know. I can't keep up with all these modern dances."

"Poor old man," Jill teased. "We'll just watch the younger generation, if you want, and only join in the slow dances."

"Suits me," Jake said as they passed into the darkness of the disco.

As they walked in, the DJ put on a slow number. Jake took Jill into his arms, holding her very closely. "Now this is the kind of dancing I'm good at," he whispered into her ear. "The kind where you don't have to move your feet."

They stood there together, swaying gently and hardly moving, while the room vibrated to the pulsing beat of a bass. Jill could feel Jake's heart beating against hers. It felt so wonderful to be close to him, to feel his arms around her, her cheek against his, his hair, soft and sweet smelling, tickling her nose. *I could stay like this forever,* she thought. *Why can't it always be this way?*

The dance finished, and a loud rock number

began. Jake made her laugh imitating some of the more violent dancers. They danced a bit more until Jake made it clear that he had had enough noise for one evening. "I really must be getting old," he said as they came out. "I used to love that stuff when I was in high school."

"Right—you're so decrepit," Jill said, teasing him. "Past your prime at twenty-one. Nothing to look forward to but Social Security."

"Oh, I wouldn't say that," Jake said softly. "I still have a few interests in life."

Jill turned and looked out the window. "Oh, wow," she said. "Look at the moon out there. It's almost full. Isn't it beautiful? Let's go out on the balcony." She dragged the protesting Jake behind her. For a moment they stood silently looking at the scene below them—the silver slopes stretching away into shadow, trees sparkling like those in store window displays, the silence complete except for the barest whisper of wind. Small, white puffs of breath hung briefly in the cold air, then dissolved away into the night.

"It's very beautiful," Jake agreed. "It's almost too beautiful, don't you think? Like a scene out of Walt Disney or something. You almost expect a couple of rabbits and a few baby deer to come dancing out of the forest."

"You're a cynic, Jake Randall," Jill said.

"And you are a hopeless romantic," he countered.

"I suppose I am," Jill said. "I suppose I want

real life to be like a Walt Disney movie, with the fawns dancing around and the handsome prince kissing me in the moonlight."

"Well, the last part can be easily arranged," Jake said, taking her into his arms and kissing her. Then he released her and held her away from him, looking down into her face. "Now could we please go inside again?" he asked. "Much as I love kissing you, I don't want our lips to get frozen together, nor do I want to be attacked by creeping frostbite."

"I suppose I'll never be able to convert you to a romantic," Jill said as they pushed open the swinging doors again.

"I must be partly romantic," Jake said. "Or I'd never have been interested in you in the first place. Now that we've kissed in the moonlight, may we please go kiss somewhere warmer—like my room?"

Jill looked down at her wrist. "Oh, heavens, is that the time?" she stammered. "Jake, I really have to go. My roommate will wonder what has happened to me. She gets worried really easily, you know, and besides, I'm tired. I've been working since eight this morning. You do understand, don't you?"

"I guess so," Jake said uncertainly. "Oh, well, you'd better go, if you want to. I'll see you tomorrow, Jill." Then he turned and strode down the hall, his boots tapping on the polished slate.

FIFTEEN

"So, did you have a terrific time last night?" Toni asked as Jill shook her awake the next morning. "I'm sorry I couldn't stay awake to ask you about it last night, but I was really wiped out. I don't think hard work agrees with me. Brandt was pretty tired, too, after the first full day's shooting, so we both collapsed around ten. So tell me all about it—or not all of it if you don't want to."

"I had a good time," Jill said. "Jake took me to dinner in the restaurant, and I ate a lot of real food—not hamburgers or chili. Then we danced in the disco for a while. It was a good evening."

"Great," Toni said, grabbing her robe and flinging it around her. "Is it my imagination, or is the floor of this room an ice-skating rink? I don't know how they expect us to perform our duties when all our limbs are frozen solid."

"That's exactly what Jake said," Jill commented.

"He didn't understand why our rooms have to be so terrible when the guest rooms are so cozy."

"Yes, they really are cozy, aren't they?" Toni said, smiling to herself. "Some of the most expensive ones actually have their own fireplaces. Of course, Brandt's doesn't. Does Jake's?"

"I—er, didn't go up to Jake's room," Jill said, opening the closet to take out her clothes.

"Oh," Toni said. "So what are your plans for today? I can't get over it—two full days of no work. Brandt says I can come up and watch the shooting if I behave myself. I don't know what he means by that, do you? But he mumbled something about knocking cameras over and tripping the director. He seems to think I'm clumsy. Where he got that idea I don't know. Anyway, Jill, I'll be up on the mountain with Brandt all day, so I'll be completely out of your hair. You can have all the time in the world to be alone with Jake. Come up here to the room if you want. I won't disturb you."

"Uh, thanks," Jill said, selecting a light blue fuzzy sweater to go with her dark blue ski overalls. "But I think Jake and I will be out all day anyway. He wants me to take him on the grand tour, so I thought we'd ski this morning and try out the cross-country course this afternoon."

Toni snorted. "Are you turning into a physical fitness nut?" she asked. "What happened to good old-fashioned sitting by the fire and sipping hot chocolate?"

"We might have time for that, too," Jill said. "In

fact, I've got a great idea. Why don't we get together for hot chocolate this evening? You've never met Jake and I hardly know Brandt, but I think we'd all get along well."

"Sure, if you want to," Toni said. "But you'd better put some rum in the hot chocolate. Brandt and I will be frozen to the bone after standing on a windy mountainside all day, watching a mechanical monster come around the crags."

"It sounds like fun," Jill said. "We'll have to go see the movie together—then we can laugh when everybody else in the audience screams."

"So, do you want the bathroom first, or shall I take it?" Toni demanded. "You mustn't keep Jake waiting, you know. If you want to fit in all that skiing and cross-country stuff, you'd better get an early start."

After Toni had gone, bounding down the hall with noisy strides to meet Brandt, Jill was left alone, putting on her ski boots. *I wish I knew what to do*, she thought, looking in the closet mirror at her pale face with the copper-colored hair spilling down around it. *Jake is wonderful and I don't want to lose him, but I think he expects more than I can cope with. I can't keep stalling forever. I'd really like to talk it all out with him, but I'd be too embarrassed.* She clicked her boots shut and stood up, feeling the strange pinching of the hard plastic around her feet. *I guess I'll just have to follow yesterday's plan.*

The night before had not really been planned at all. The idea of going dancing and then looking at the moon had just come to her as she searched desperately for reasons not to go to Jake's room. But now a real plan was beginning to form in her mind. If she could keep Jake busy enough, if she could tire him out on the ski slopes, then she wouldn't have to spend the evening fighting him off. It was the only way she could see of not driving Jake away and yet not encouraging him either. *And it just might work,* she told herself as she climbed down the hall to meet him.

Jake stopped in a shower of white spray and leaned on his ski poles while he waited for Jill to join him. She pushed her goggles up on her head and smiled at him. "That was wonderful, wasn't it? The best run we've had all morning."

Jake nodded. "It was fun," he said. "I liked the part at the top where there was a sheer drop and you felt as if you were on a roller coaster. The rest was kind of tame."

"Not for me," Jill said. "You're a much better skier than I am, Jake, because that slope was tough for me. But if you really found it boring, I'll be brave and go up to Siberia with you. That's the most challenging run. Do you want to try it?"

Jake pushed his goggles farther back on his forehead. "I can't move another muscle," he complained. "Don't you feel tired yet?"

"Oh, no," Jill lied. "I could keep going for hours."

Jake stared at her suspiciously. "Why did you

132

keep it a secret from me that you were a super-jock in disguise?" he demanded. "You know I can't stand fitness freaks."

"Oh, but, Jake," Jill pleaded, "you don't understand. I've been up here nearly a week, and this is the first chance I've had to go skiing. It's hard to stand there serving plates heaped with chili and cornbread and hear everyone talk about the great runs they've had. And it's such a gorgeous day. I want to make the most of it."

"If you make much more of it, you won't be able to move a muscle tomorrow," Jake said. "There's such a thing as overdoing it, you know, and you are not exactly the world's greatest athlete."

"I am on the water polo team," Jill said crushingly. "Which is one step more athletic than you."

"That water polo team is a joke," Jake said. "But I don't want to argue about it. I don't know about you, but I'm dying of thirst. Let's go have lunch, please. Then we can decide if you are suicidal enough to want to try some more slopes this afternoon."

"I think maybe you're right," Jill said as they unsnapped their bindings and left their skis in the rack outside the snack terrace. "Maybe we'd be crazy to do too much this afternoon."

"Now you're making sense," Jake said.

"You said you wanted the grand tour," Jill continued, "so one of my friends down in the equipment shop suggested we do the cross-country circuit. It's a cross-country ski course that takes you in a loop around the lodge and back."

"But I've never tried cross-country skiiing," Jake complained. "Isn't it strenuous?"

"Nothing like downhill," Jill said. "And we'd take it very gently. It would give you the best view of the whole resort, and we could get a great tan, too."

"Okay, I guess so," Jake said, sighing. "But am I ever going to get some time alone with you?"

"It gets dark early," Jill said. "And that leaves us a whole long evening. I can see now that you let yourself get out of shape at college, and I'm going to have to get you fit again."

Jake eyed her suspiciously. "You're not the United States Marines in disguise, are you?" he asked. "Oh, well, we 'd better go eat a huge lunch packed with protein so we can drag ourselves around the cross-country course."

SIXTEEN

The light had faded to a dusky pink as Jill and Jake staggered up the last slope toward the lodge again.

"Doesn't it look warm and inviting, with the smoke curling up against the evening sky like that?" Jill asked. "Exactly like a Christmas card."

"Hmmm," Jake said. "I'm too busy concentrating on putting one ski in front of the other to notice. And I'm also saving up enough energy to punch out that friend of yours who told you that this was a gentle loop around the lodge. He failed to mention that this was a ten-mile loop, up and down a few major mountains."

"But the views were terrific, weren't they?" Jill piped up brightly, even though she was finding it equally difficult to push her skis forward. "I loved that section of pine forest. It smelled so fresh and tangy."

"I like the smell I'm getting now much better," Jake said, looking up for the first time. "The warm, inviting aroma of french fries frying and hamburgers sizzling. That's my kind of smell."

"Well, you can have food any minute now," Jill said. "Let's take our skis off and turn them in to the rental shop. I'll go up to change and meet you down in the snack bar later. Okay?"

"Okay," Jake said. He learned across on his skis and gave Jill an unexpected kiss. "Sorry if I was an old grouch," he said. "I guess I had my fill of skiing up at the cabin. And I hope you got your fill today, too."

"I've really enjoyed it," Jill said. "Especially being with you."

"Tell you what," Jake said, rubbing his nose against her cheek. "Tomorrow, let's be together in less strenuous surroundings—or else I'm not going to hold out for a week." He tried to straighten up, felt his skis slipping, and toppled over sideways. He lay there in the snow glaring up at a laughing Jill.

"See, what did I tell you?" she asked, helping him up. "You really are getting old. Tomorrow I'll push you around in a wheelchair."

"Actually, I'd like that," he said, pushing down with his pole to unsnap the front binding. "Boy, it feels good to get rid of those things. That's the last time I'm going cross-country skiing. Anyone who tells you that it's easier than downhill is lying!" He swung both pairs of skis onto his shoulder and stalked off toward the rental shop. "I'll see you in a little while," he called back. "I'd jump into a hot bath if I were you. It'll prevent your muscles from stiffening up."

Jill watched him hobble up the steps, then went inside, her own legs trembling violently as she climbed the steps. "A hot bath," she said with a sigh of content. "What a great idea. And maybe I could lie down for ten minutes before I meet him for dinner. I'm beginning to think my idea of keeping Jake occupied is as crazy as something Toni would have dreamed up!"

She flung open the door of her room and stood open-mouthed with amazement in the doorway.

"Now you've just made me miss a gate!" Toni yelled.

Jill continued to stand and stare. "What exactly are you doing?" she demanded.

Toni had pushed both the beds back against the wall and was standing crouched, with her skis on, in the middle of the floor. She was swaying from side to side and swinging her poles wildly.

"What does it look like I'm doing?" Toni asked without stopping.

"It looks as if you are trying to ski down the middle of a vinyl floor."

"Correct," Toni said. "Now please don't interrupt me. I've only got two more gates before I finish this race."

Jill shut the door behind her and watched in amused puzzlement as Toni swayed some more and then brought her arms up in a sign of victory, which sent the overhead light swinging dangerously. "How about that?" she asked. "Under two minutes on the first run."

"Have you finally flipped?" Jill asked. "Or is there a logical explanation to all this?"

"Perfectly logical," Toni said. "I'm practicing for tomorrow's slalom."

"You're what?" Jill shrieked.

"Tomorrow's slalom," Toni repeated. "I was just practicing."

"You can't be serious," Jill stammered. "No way are you entering a ski race."

"And why not?" Toni demanded.

"Why not? Because, if my memory serves me right, you only mastered the snow plow a short time ago."

"It's okay," Toni said calmly. "It's not a real ski race, and anyway I've been studying all afternoon." She leaned over toward the nearest bed and lifted up an open book.

"The technique of ski racing," Jill read. "Toni, you can't teach yourself to ski by reading a book."

"I don't see why not," Toni said. "It's all a question of knowing where to put your weight. See, when I'm approaching a gate from the left I lean over like this, and my poles come out like this— whoops sorry," she exclaimed as she hit Jill across the waist. "I've talked myself through the whole course, Jill."

"But, Toni, use your head," Jill pleaded. "You're currently standing on a flat floor. It's easy to shift your weight from foot to foot when the floor is not dropping away from you. I should know. When I came down Upper Snowfire this morning, all I could do was lean as far forward as possible, hold my breath, and pray. There was no way I could have shifted my weight."

"It's all a matter of positive thinking," Toni said, consulting her book again and going back to her swaying. "Just a minute, I've got to get that part with the moguls right. I'm not quite sure how to land again."

"On your seat, I would think," Jill said dryly. "Really, Toni, you don't get any less crazy as you get older. I can see you now in a wheelchair race when you're ninety-five. Would you mind telling me what brought on this sudden passionate interest in skiing? You've never wanted to be a champion in any sport before. In fact, you used to laugh at the girls who were super-jocks in school."

"It's not the sport itself I'm interested in," Toni said, bending down to unsnap her bindings.

"Well, this time it can't be a boy, not with Brandt here."

"It's only my whole future," Toni said grandly. "This could turn my whole life around, Jill."

Jill sank down on the nearest bed. Her legs, which had been getting progressively weaker, suddenly would not hold her up any longer. "Go on," she said suspiciously. Toni had that wild gleam in her eye that often meant she was coming up with one of her wild ideas. And because those ideas often included Jill, Jill had a right to be suspicious.

"It's the movie," Toni said excitedly. "Today I was on the set, and it was so exciting. I knew right away that the only thing I want to do in the entire world is act in movies. And now the perfect chance has come up. I heard the director tell Brandt that they're going to use some of the girl skiers at the resort for extras. See, the monster will interrupt an international ski race, and people are supposed to come flying down the mountain with the monster close behind. This is going to be *it*, Jill. Other girls will be able to ski faster than I can, but I'm an actress. The look of terror on my face will be the best, and the director will look at the rushes and say, 'Who was that girl? She only flashed across the screen for a couple of seconds, but her look of terror made the whole movie. I must get her to work for me again!'"

"So you think you'll be able to come flying down the mountain tomorrow?" Jill asked. "After one afternoon of floor practice?"

"I'll manage," Toni said, looking up from the boots she was taking off. "I've got to, Jill. I can't afford to let this chance slip away."

Jill looked at her wryly. "I don't know if you've seen the slalom course, but, believe me, if you try coming down it, your look of terror will not be an act—it'll be genuine." She reached out and touched Toni's shoulder. "You might get hurt, Toni," she said gently. "It's not worth taking a risk like that for a small part in a movie."

"Have you any idea how difficult it is to get into movies?" Toni asked. "To get hired, you have to belong to a union, but to belong to a union you have to have a job in a movie. Do you see the problem?"

"Of course," Jill said. "But you do have connections now. Brandt knows people in the business. I bet if you asked him he'd find you something that wasn't so dangerous."

Toni made a face. "Brandt thinks I should take things one step at time," she said. "He thinks I should finish college first and get some good acting training before I try to do any professional work." She looked at Jill and sighed. "He doesn't realize that I'm getting older by the minute. By the time I'm discovered, I won't be able to play cute young heroines anymore. I'll have to be someone's middle-aged housekeeper."

Jill had to laugh. "You are funny sometimes," she said. "With your face you're going to be able to play young heroines until you're fifty. And Brandt is absolutely right. You do need the training first."

"But when I go for a job you know what they're going to say, don't you?" Toni sighed. "They're going to say, 'I'm sorry, you don't have any experience yet.' I think my way is much better. I'll go on with my training, I promise, but I'll be in movies, too. After all, Jill, I've got to know if I'm wasting my time, don't I? I might not have a face that's right for movies, and I'd like to know that before I waste four years studying theater arts."

"Oh, I wouldn't worry if I were you," Jill said, leaning back on the bed and feeling her aching muscles quiver as they came in contact with the mattress. "There will always be a horror movie with a role for you. You know, the thing that oozes up from the middle of the bog or sucks blood from the veins of a spaceman."

Toni looked for something to throw but couldn't find anything soft, so she waved her ski pole menacingly. "You're supposed to be my friend, remember?" she said grouchily. "You're supposed to encourage me."

"Not encourage you to kill yourself," Jill said. "I care about you, Toni. I don't want you lying in a hospital for the rest of your life with a severed spinal cord."

"That won't happen to me," Toni said. "You know what I'm like. When I fall, I bounce. Anyway, I'm not going to fall. I am determined to ski down that course tomorrow, and nothing is going to stop me."

SEVENTEEN

Jill and Jake did not go to the restaurant that night. Instead they were both content with hamburgers and fries at the snack bar. At least Jake was content. He wolfed down three hamburgers and declared that he was still hungry. Jill was so exhausted that her arms trembled violently every time she lifted her hamburger to her mouth. This made her feel so embarrassed that she hardly ate anything. Jake had completely recovered from their strenuous day and made jokes all through the meal.

"Promise me one thing," he said to Jill as he helped her up from the table. "No dancing to-night—okay? My legs wouldn't hold up."

Jill smiled. "Definitely no dancing," she said. "I can't even walk as far as the disco."

"So I finally get you to myself for an evening?" Jake asked. "I can't believe it. You mean there's no indoor skating rink you'd like to try? They don't have a jogging track in the basement, or a racquet-ball court?"

"We *are* at a ski resort, you know, and until you came along all I had seen of it was the kitchen and a few hallways."

"Okay, you're right," he said, putting his arm around her shoulder and pulling her close to him. "But now we're going to have a wonderful cozy evening, just the two of us. Correct?"

"Correct," Jill said, turning her face up to be kissed. They walked out of the snack bar and into the main lobby. It looked especially inviting that night with the firelight reflected off the copper fireplace hood, throwing a rosy glow onto the faces gathered around it. Jill and Jake had hardly walked a few paces when Jill grabbed his arm. "Oh, look, there are my friends Toni and Brandt," she said. "They're dying to meet you. We'd better just go over and say a few words." Before he could protest, Jill grabbed his hand and dragged him to the table in the corner.

"Well, hi there, strangers," she said brightly.

Toni smiled up at Jake. "So this is the famous Jake," she said. "Hi, I'm Toni, and this is Brandt." Everybody shook hands.

"So you're responsible for all the equipment up on the slopes," Jake said pleasantly. "We nearly skied over a cable this morning. Come to think of it, we were dumb, Jill. We should have pretended not to notice the cable and skied over it, then broken a leg and sued the movie company."

Jill laughed. "Thanks very much, but I'd prefer not to break my leg," she said. "Anyway, you can't blame Brandt for where they put cables. He's the assistant director, so he's only involved with the artistic side of things."

Brandt snorted. "If you call holding the sunscreen for the director's secretary the artistic side," he said. "That's about as artistic as I've gotten so far. I do have to arrange the avalanche later this week, which should be fun," he said. "But most of the time I just hang around. It'll get better once we're back in the studios doing the voices, but right now I feel like the new kid on the block whom nobody trusts."

"You mean they're not going to trust you with the tryouts the director was talking about today?" Toni asked hopefully.

"Oh, those," Brandt said. "Big deal. I get to choose some skiers to flee from the monster. I hardly call that artistic. If they make it down the course I hire them. Unless they weigh two hundred pounds!"

Jill looked down at the table. "Is that hot chocolate you two are drinking?" she asked. "I've been here all week and still haven't tried the hot chocolate yet."

"It's very good," Brandt said. "Would you like to join us?"

Toni touched his arm. "Oh, I'm sure they—" she said, but Jill was already sitting down. "Thanks," she said. "A cup of hot chocolate would be a perfect ending for that meal, wouldn't it, Jake?"

"If you say so," Jake said, pulling out the chair beside her and sitting down.

The cups of hot chocolate were ordered and served. Jill sipped hers slowly while the talk flowed around her. Toni asked Jake questions about Rosemont, and Jake gave amusing descriptions of weird professors and Jill's water polo team. The warmth of the fire made Jill feel drowsy. She fought to keep herself awake, drifting in and out of consciousness, but snapped awake when she heard Toni say, "Well, we should get going, shouldn't we, Brandt? I'm sure Jill and Jake don't want to waste a whole evening telling us stories about Rosemont. I bet they're glad to be away from the place for a while."

She stood up to go. Jill put her hand on Toni's arm and forced her down again. "But you have to hear this one first. It's so funny, and Jake tells it so well. "You know, that cross-country team we got together to run against the University of Oregon. Jake wrote this witty article about it for the newspaper. Rosemont challenged Oregon to a cross-country race. 'The Great Race,' we called it. It was supposed to be a joke, really, because Oregon is one of the best track schools in the country. We thought they wouldn't even bother with a team as bad as ours! Only somewhere along the way it got serious, and we found that they were sending a real cross-country team to compete with us. So tell them what happened, Jake, and how we tried to sabotage it. . . ."

Jake took over the story and had them all

laughing as he described how the Rosemont students rigged the course so that they ran five miles less and the Oregon runners got all the hills. When he had finished, Jill touched Toni's arm. "That reminds me about that time at school—"

"What time?" Toni asked.

"You know," Jill insisted. "When we had that new PE teacher and he made us do that fitness program. Tell them about that—"

"Well, okay," Toni said. "It wasn't as funny as Jake's story, though."

"Oh, I thought it was funny," Jill said. "Especially when we changed the dials on the exercise machine."

"Yeah, that was kind of funny," Toni agreed and started to tell the story. Jill leaned her head back against the knotty pine of the wall. She heard Toni's clear voice describing their campaign against the PE teacher. She closed her eyes. Toni's voice slipped farther and farther away. . . .

The next thing she knew, she heard a voice murmuring, "She's sound asleep, poor thing. You must have done too much today. She's not used to all that exercise."

"You want me to help you carry her up to your room?" Brandt's voice was asking, still far away, as if he were at the end of a tunnel. Jill knew she should wake up and say something sensible, but her limbs all felt like lead, and her jaw muscles felt frozen.

"It's okay, I can manage." She heard Jake's

voice. She felt herself being lifted up and rested her head against Jake's warm shoulder.

"I'll have to show you the way," Toni said. "Poor old Jill—I hope she's all right."

"She'll be fine when she's had a good night's sleep," Jake was saying. "I told her she was doing too much today, but she wanted to cram a week's skiing into one day. I never knew she was such a manic skier."

"Oh, yes," came Toni's voice, close to Jill's head. "She's a manic skier, all right. She doesn't think of anything but skiing all winter."

Jill wanted to laugh, but she couldn't even wake up enough to do that. She was conscious of an icy blast of air, footsteps echoing down a cold hallway, then being placed gently on a cold bed.

"I'll get her undressed," Toni said kindly. "Thanks for your help. I'm sorry—your evening got kind of wrecked, didn't it?"

"Don't worry about it, it wasn't your fault," Jake's voice said. "And, anyway, I don't feel as if I can stay awake much longer myself after all that skiing. Do you know how long ten miles of cross-country skiing is? It goes on forever. Well, good night, Toni. Nice to have met you. Tell Jill I'll see her at breakfast."

Jill heard a door closing softly, and that was the last thing she remembered until morning.

EIGHTEEN

"Oh, I'm so glad you're okay," Toni greeted Jill as she opened her eyes the next morning.

"Why shouldn't I be okay?" Jill asked, feeling slightly confused.

"Because you fell asleep in the lobby last night and nobody could wake you up. I thought you'd gotten sleeping sickness or something."

Jill propped herself up on one elbow and smiled. "You get sleeping sickness from flies in Africa," she said, "not from cross-country skiing. I was just exhausted, that's all."

"So was Jake," Toni said. "And he hinted it was all your fault that you both did too much yesterday. He said he didn't know you were such a manic skier."

"It wasn't a question of being a manic skier," Jill said, sliding out of bed and walking over to the window. "I thought he liked skiing."

"He does, but not in such large doses," Toni said, wriggling into her long underwear. "How does the weather look out there?"

"Not too good," Jill said. "It's snowing right now, and the clouds in the sky look really heavy."

"That's good," Toni said.

"You mean now they'll have to cancel the tryouts and you won't have to make a fool of yourself?" Jill asked.

"Not at all," Toni said hotly. "I mean that all that swirling snow will make it harder for Brandt to recognize me."

"It will also make it harder for you to ski down the mountain," Jill commented. "You have trouble staying upright even if the weather is perfect. How are you going to manage if you have snow swirling in your face and winds buffeting you?"

"I'll manage," Toni said. "Don't try to talk me out of this. I've made up my mind, and there's nothing you can do to make me change it."

"Okay," Jill said. "I read you. I only hope I won't have to watch as they carry your mangled body down from the mountain on a stretcher."

"Actually, Jill," Toni said cautiously, "I've got a big favor to ask—"

"No," Jill said firmly. "I will not ski the course for you."

"Not that, stupid," Toni said. "I want it to be *my* face that shows the look of terror for the camera. What I hoped you'd do is talk to Brandt—"

"About what?" Jill asked, still suspicious.

"Any old thing," Toni said impatiently. "Just be up there, chatting with him so that he won't notice me slip away and join the tryouts."

"Oh, come, on, Toni," Jill said. "You know that I hate to lie. He's bound to notice you're not there. And what am I supposed to say if he asks me where you are?"

"Say I've gone to the bathroom. Or just say you don't know, which will be the truth, because you won't know exactly where I am on the slope," Toni said. She walked over to Jill and put her hands on Jill's shoulders. "Please, Jill," she begged. "I'm not asking you to do much. Just cover for me, so that I can have a chance to ski. It means so much to me. If only I could get a part in a movie, I know some big shot director would discover me and then I'd become a big star, and I wouldn't forget you when I moved to Hollywood and had a heart-shaped swimming pool—"

"Toni Redmond," Jill said severely, "I wonder if you are ever going to grow up."

"I hope not." Toni grinned. "Just because I have dreams and ambitions while most people settle for thinking about what they're going to have for dinner. You won't let me down, will you, Jill?"

Jill sighed. "I suppose not," she said. "I don't mind talking to Brandt for you, I suppose, but I am worried about you. This is one of the craziest things you've ever done."

"Crazier than that time I tried out for the chorus line?"

"Much crazier," Jill said. "The farthest you could have fallen then was into the orchestra pit."

"Crazier than chasing Philippe all the way to France?" Toni asked.

"Just as crazy," Jill said. "And more dangerous."

"Well, I'm still going through with it," Toni said. "There's nothing you can say that will stop me."

"Oh, that I believe," Jill said. "I've tried to stop you from doing dumb things ever since you challenged the class bully to a fight back in second grade, and I haven't succeeded yet. I should have learned my lesson when the bully decided to fight me instead of you!"

"Nothing bad is going to happen to you today," Toni said. "All you have to do is watch and talk. That's not too much to ask, is it?"

"I guess not," Jill said reluctantly, opening her closet and frowning. "Now let's see. Do I have any clothing suitable for being buried in a blizzard?"

Toni was chuckling as she walked down the hall.

Jill had to admit that she admired Toni's guts—she always had. As they all rode the cable car to the upper slopes Toni chatted brightly, flirted with Jake, and snugged up to Brandt, giving no hint that she was scared. Jill, on the other hand, felt as if her stomach was tying itself into knots. She felt as if she, and not Toni, were just about to compete in a crazy ski race. Jake was also strangely quiet, answering questions in monosyllables and staring out of the gondola at the dark, brooding pine woods below them.

When Jill asked him once if something was wrong, he answered in a tight voice. "Wrong? Why should something be wrong?"

"Because you seem kind of angry," Jill said. "Did I do something to upset you?"

"What makes you think that?" Jake answered. "I'm really looking forward to a full day of standing in a blizzard."

"But you said you wanted to watch some of the shooting," Jill said. "And Toni invited us to come along today. We couldn't very well turn down her invitation, could we?"

Jake shrugged his shoulders. Jill nestled her head against his sleeve. "Look, we don't have to stick around all day," she said. "As soon as Toni—I mean, as soon as we've been up there for a while, we can come down again."

Jake did not answer. Jill stared out at the snow, feeling dangerously close to crying. Why did life always have to be so complicated? The last thing in the world she wanted to do was make Jake angry and drive him away.

The gondola swung itself into its dock. Its cargo of skiers grabbed their equipment and pushed off onto the slopes, leaving the four of them standing on the windy mountainside.

"Now we have to trek up that hill to where the cameras are," Brandt said. "When I agreed to work on this movie, I had no idea what I was letting myself in for. Have you girls noticed any Saint Bernard dogs hanging around the lodge? I have a feeling they're going to have to come looking for us before today is over."

"You should have brought some skis like I told you," Toni said to him. "If a blizzard starts blowing and the gondola won't run, the rest of us will just ski down to the bottom and you'll be stuck up here."

"And I told you I don't know anything about skiing," Brandt said. "I want to reach the bottom in one piece."

"Then how can you expect to pick the right skiers for your movie?" Toni demanded.

"To be perfectly honest with you, I don't really care who I pick," Brandt said. "I was just told to select ten girls. The way the weather is now, I think I'll just call out the first ten names on the list and hire them."

"But that's not fair!" Toni blurted out. "I mean, you might have someone who signed up late but is the best skier of all. Or she may not be the greatest skier, but she might be the one who's the best actress!"

"I don't need actresses, Toni," Brandt said. "They just have to ski down a mountain, very fast, looking over their shoulders in terror as a monster comes after them. You don't need Meryl Streep for that!"

"Well, we're all going to make sure you pick the best ten, aren't we, Jill?" Toni asked. "We won't let you get off the mountain until you've given all the girls a chance."

"Toni Redmond, fighter for justice and equality," Jake said, grinning at Jill. Jill was glad he didn't seem to be angry anymore. She was beginning to wish she had had time to let Jake in on Toni's crazy secret. He was very observant and likely to make some comment if she disappeared or suddenly came skiing past them. Jill pulled her wool hat down farther over her ears and wished the day would hurry up and end.

They took up positions on a flat area below the top of the mountain where a finish gate had been rigged up. A couple of cameras were already in position, and an efficient woman with a clipboard was scurrying about like an animated wind-up mouse. "Oh, there you are, Brandt, honey," she said, hurring over to him. "We're all ready to start, and we need to get through as quickly as possible because the weather is supposed to close in later— whatever that means!"

"It probably means we won't be able to find our way down to the lodge again," Brandt said grimly. "Oh, well, let's get it over with. Tell them to send down the first girl and get her name when she arrives here."

A walkie-talkie crackled, and a small red shape came speeding down the mountain. As the snow flurries subsided, they could clearly make out the shape of a skier in a red one-piece ski suit, hurtling downward, bent forward in a racing position. She reached a large bump, took off, flew, landed and swooshed to a halt close to Brandt's group.

"She can ski all right, but she has about as much personality as a flying tomato," Brandt commented.

Another girl followed, then another. Each of them was a skiing robot—able to perfectly negotiate a difficult course while making it seem as easy as the bunny slope.

"You see, what did I tell you?" Toni whispered to Jill. "None of them are even thinking of acting. That's why I'll be so outstanding. This is where I make my move—"

"But what do I tell Brandt?" Jill hissed.

"Tell him I went to the bathroom!" Toni whispered and slipped behind Jill's back.

A fourth skier came down—an enormous girl with arms like tree trunks. Brandt turned to the others. "Maybe not this one," he said. "We need to be able to tell the monster from his victims." He grinned, then looked surprised. "Where's Toni?" he asked.

"I think she went to the bathroom," Jill stammered.

Brandt sighed. "That girl. She's always looking for the bathroom. When she writes her autobiography, it will be called *Bathrooms I Have Known!*"

Another skier came toward them, dressed head to toe in black, her face covered by huge goggles.

"We needed to see your expression," Brandt called to her as she stopped beside them.

"You're kidding," the girl said, pushing her

goggles back on her forehead. "You try skiing that course with no goggles on in a snowstorm. You have to be able to see where you're going, you know!"

"Well, this next girl isn't wearing goggles," a cameraman commented, looking up from his zoom lens.

"She's crazy," the girl said dryly. "It's really snowing hard up there. She won't be able to see the course."

Jill looked up and picked out the flash of Toni's yellow parka through the swirling snow. She found herself holding her breath. Her heart was thumping alarmingly, and her hands were clenched into tight fists.

"Have you got her on camera two?" Brandt asked.

"Yeah, I've got her," the cameraman replied. "You want some closeups? She's kind of cute!"

"Sure, let's see," Brandt said.

"Hey, wait a minute!" the cameraman exclaimed. "I've lost her again. Where'd she go?"

"Did she fall?" Brandt asked, shielding his eyes as he peered upward.

"No, there she is," Jake said. "What does she think she's doing? She's heading straight for those pine trees."

"She obviously didn't see that sharp left-hand turn," Brandt said. "I hope she'll be okay. I feel bad that I was the one who told them not to wear goggles!"

"She's okay," Jake commented. "Look, she's realized her mistake. She's coming back toward us."

"I hope she notices us," the cameraman replied. "She's heading straight in our direction!"

Jill watched in horror as the brave yellow shape came hurtling down the steep slope toward them. She was moving so fast that she was almost a blur. Above the *whirr* of cameras you could hear the *swish* of her skis.

"She hasn't seen us," the cameraman yelled. "Wave your arms so that she notices us!"

Several pairs of arms waved frantically. Jill could not make hers move. She felt as if she was paralyzed with fright. The skier still hadn't changed course. She was heading down at an impossibly steep angle, coming straight toward them.

"Move the camera out of the way!" Brandt yelled. "The crazy idiot is going to run right into us!"

The whole movie unit struggled into action, flinging themselves in all directions, with much more realistic looks of terror on their faces than any of the skiers had shown.

Jake grabbed at Jill. "Get out of the way," he yelled. But he didn't have to worry. Just above their site was a large mogul. Toni hit it at full speed, became airborne, and soared over their astonished heads. Jill had a momentary glimpse of Toni's face—wide-eyed with terror as she looked down at the shapes below her—before she dropped to the ground again. She landed awkwardly, bounced, fell, and rolled over and over again like a bright yellow ball.

They all dropped their equipment and rushed to her. Jill reached her at the same time as Brandt. She heard his horrified "Toni!" as she dropped to her knees beside her friend. As she heard her name, Toni opened her eyes. "Hi, Brandt," she said, giving him a weak smile. "I bet I had the best expression of terror, didn't I?"

NINETEEN

Toni lay between crisp white sheets. Her face was terribly pale, and her hand, resting above the sheet, seemed as frail and transparent as a butterfly wing. Jill caught her breath as she stood there in the doorway, looking down at her friend. Toni's eyes were closed, and her face looked so peaceful that for a horrible moment Jill wondered if she were dead. But as she moved toward the bed, Toni's eyes opened and she gave a weak grin.

"How are you feeling?" Jill asked gently.

"Terrific," Toni said. "As if I'm floating. It was that pain medication they gave me when they wrapped my ankle. I hate to think about how it's going to feel when the stuff wears off."

Jill rattled a little bottle sitting on the small table beside her bed. "There's more here. You can keep floating all night if you want to."

Toni looked confused. "Why, what time is it?" she asked.

"About seven in the evening."

Toni's eyes shot wide open. "But I don't remember anything since this morning. Have I been asleep that long?"

Jill nodded. "We brought you back from the hospital around four. You were semi-awake then, and you gave Brandt and Jake instructions about the correct way to carry you all the way up the stairs."

Toni smiled. "I sort of remember that."

"Then I asked you if you wanted something to eat or drink," Jill said. "And you said you were starving and you'd like a hamburger, fries, and a milk shake. But by the time I brought the food, you were sound asleep, and you've slept ever since."

"Good," Toni said. "I wondered why I felt so relaxed and rested. I obviously needed an excuse for a good long nap."

Jill sat down on the edge of her bed. "You are amazing, you know that?" she asked. "When I saw you fall this morning, I thought that you must have hurt yourself really badly. You actually flew through the air!"

Toni grinned at the memory of it. "I've always wanted to play Peter Pan," she said. "Now someone'll have to give me the part because I'll be the only one with experience."

"I don't think you have any idea just how lucky you are, Toni Redmond!" Jill said severely. "You could be lying here paralyzed now, instead of just having a sprained ankle. The rest of us are feeling much worse than you are! We were all shivering so badly when we got to the hospital that the nurse said we were suffering from exposure and made us lie down with blankets over us."

"I'm sorry if I scared you," Toni said. "I went the wrong way up there. I couldn't see a thing with the snow blowing in my eyes, and suddenly I was heading for this pine forest. So I managed to change direction—I'm not sure how—I just leaned as hard as I could on my left ski and finally I came around. But then I saw that I wasn't heading for the pine trees anymore, I was heading straight for the cameras." She chuckled. "If I hadn't been so terrified I guess it would have been funny. Everyone was grabbing everything and scattering all over the place!"

"And just think what might have happened if you hadn't become airborne and had hit some people," Jill reminded her. "I really hope you've finally learned a lesson—maybe next time you'll think twice before you pull any more crazy stunts!"

"I'll try," Toni said, smiling. "It's just that I get these ideas, Jill, and they seem so possible to me—"

"And so impossible to everyone else," Jill said. "I hope you stick with Brandt for a long time. He cares a lot about you, and he's a very sensible person. If anyone can make you grow up, he can."

Toni's eyes crinkled up at the corners as she smiled. "He's really great, isn't he?"

"Really great," Jill said. "You should have seen him sitting beside your bed, holding your hand while you snored."

"I did not snore!" Toni said emphatically, then asked, "Did I?"

"A little," Jill said. "But we figured that was because of the anesthetic. Brandt had to go to a meeting a little while ago, but he didn't want to leave you. I kept trying to reassure him that you'd only sprained your ankle and that you were very, very tough, but I practically had to push him out the door."

Toni smiled, "I really love him, Jill. I don't think I've ever felt this way about anyone else. Other guys have made my heart beat fast whenever I thought of them, but Brandt makes me feel warm all over when I think of him. When I'm with him, I don't feel that I have to pretend to be anyone. I can just relax and be me—and that's a good feeling, Jill."

"I know," Jill said. "I used to feel like that with Craig—" She broke off in midsentence.

Toni looked at her sharply. "Do you still miss him?" she asked.

Jill toyed with the starched corner of the sheet. "I don't know, Toni. Sometimes I think I've finally gotten over him, but then other times I can't stop myself from thinking about him. I guess it'll take awhile before I'm over him completely. We were together for a long time."

"So Jake hasn't completely taken his place in your heart?" Toni asked.

"Jake—" Jill said hesitantly—"Jake is different. Jake makes me feel like I've never felt before, Toni. It's exciting to be with him, but I'm not quite sure of myself when we're together."

"Is that why you've been running away from him ever since he arrived?" Toni asked, turning over awkwardly to face Jill.

"I haven't been running away," Jill said hotly.

"Disco dancing his first evening? Ten miles of cross-country skiing his second day? That sounds to me like you're trying to keep him at arm's length."

"I guess you're right," Jill said at last. "I thought that if I kept him busy enough—"

"He wouldn't have the time or energy for what's really on his mind," Toni finished for her. "Is he coming on too strong—or did you decide when you saw him again that you didn't like him as much as you thought you did?"

"I don't know," Jill said hesitantly. "The whole trouble is that I really like him. When he's kissing me I feel as if—as if there's a big warm bubble growing inside my head. But he's older than I am, Toni, and he's used to more, I guess. And I'm not. Toni, how do you know when you're ready for sex?"

"If you have to ask that question, then you're not," Toni said firmly. "When you are ready for it, it will seem like the most natural thing in the world. It did to me. You know, I spent my first eighteen years fighting off guys in cars and on sofas, and then I met Brandt. I suppose you just have to meet the right person at the right time."

"But how will I know when it's the right time?" Jill said. "Sometimes I think I'm about ten years behind the rest of the world. It's all my parents' fault. They kept hammering these strict moral ideas into me!"

Toni laughed. "It's not your parents, dummy. It's the way you are. You hate to lie, you hate to hurt other people, you hate to do anything that you feel is morally wrong. It may be that you're the type of person who wants to wait to have sex until you get married."

"Or at least until I'm convinced that the person is the right one for me," Jill said. "I guess I'm afraid of Jake's playboy reputation. I'm really attracted to him, but I'm scared that I'll get too involved, and then he'll get tired of me, and I'll feel let down and guilty."

"I understand how you feel," Toni said. "So just don't let yourself be pressured into anything you don't want."

"I'm not being pressured," Jill said. "At least, not in the way you think. Jake is behaving like a perfect gentleman, but I can't help feeling that he didn't come up here just for the skiing."

"Then I think you two should have a talk," Toni said. "So you both know where you stand."

"You're right," Jill said. "But it isn't easy for me to talk about things like this—especially not with a guy. Also—" She broke off.

Toni looked up and saw her face. "Also you're afraid he'll go away and won't come back," she

165

finished for her. "Would it hurt you that much if you lost him? And I don't mean just your pride—I mean really hurt inside."

Jill nodded.

"Then go for it!" Toni said.

Jill laughed uneasily. "I wish it were as easy as that," she said. "I've got eighteen years of being a good little girl to stamp out. Sometimes I have the horrible feeling that I might die an old maid."

"Don't worry about it," Toni said. "I'm going to be rich and famous—and adored by sexy guys. I'll keep you supplied with wool for your knitting and food for your cats!"

Jill glared down at her. "If you weren't lying there with sore bones I'd throw something at you," she said.

Toni giggled. Jill laughed, too. "Anyway, I'm glad you feel well enough to be your normal obnoxious self," she said. "You really scared me today, Toni Redmond, and I hope I never have to live through something like that again."

"I don't know about that," Toni said. "I've been thinking that I might be able to get a job as a movie stunt woman. It's not everyone who can fly through the air—"

"But most stunt people do the stunts deliberately," Jill said. "They only take off when the script tells them to. With you we would never know when the next stunt was coming! Now you'd better get some rest. I promised I'd meet Jake down in the lounge. Do you want me to bring you up some food first?"

"I don't think I feel like eating right now," Toni said. "Talking to you made me feel pretty tired again. It's not easy being Dear Abby. In fact, I think I'll . . ."

"You'll what?" Jill asked gently, but Toni didn't answer. She was already asleep.

TWENTY

"How is she?" Jake asked, getting up from his leather armchair by the fire as Jill walked into the lounge.

"She's fine," Jill said. "I told you Toni was tough, and she really is. Apart from being drowsy from the pain killers, she's back to being her old self."

"She's lucky," Jake said, shaking his head in disbelief. "When I saw her go sailing over our heads like that, I thought she'd break her neck or something."

"So did I," Jill agreed. "Even Toni doesn't usually do such spectacular things. But I've left her sleeping peacefully, and she'll probably be up and around in the morning. Do you feel like having dinner yet?"

"Not really," Jake said, looking hard at Jill. "I feel like talking."

"Okay," Jill said. "You want to sit down here by the fire?"

"No," Jake said firmly. "I want to talk up in my room."

"Oh," Jill said uneasily. "Well, okay, I guess—"

"I want to talk to you in private, Jill," Jake said. "Not in a lounge where half the world can hear, not out on the ski slopes or in the dining room or next to Toni and Brandt. I want to be alone with you for once, do you understand that?"

"Sure," Jill said. "I understand that. We don't seem to have had much chance to be alone the past couple of days."

"I've noticed," Jake said. He took her arm and led her firmly down through the lobby and across to the elevator. They didn't speak while the elevator rose to the third floor, or while they walked silently down the thickly carpeted hallway. Jake took out his key and let them in.

"Wow, this is really nice," Jill commented, trying to sound bright and cheerful, but feeling herself trembling inside from the thought of what might be coming next. "You even have a little fridge! Do you have any Cokes in it, by any chance?"

"Not now, Jill," Jake said. "Let's talk first. You see, there are things that I don't understand. I have to find out what's going on."

"What do you mean?" Jill asked cautiously.

"You know exactly what I mean," Jake said, taking both her hands. "I'm talking about us. What is the problem?"

"Problem?" Jill asked shakily. She knew she was sounding like a parrot, but she couldn't think of anything else to say.

"Oh, come on, Jill," Jake said angrily. "I'm not exactly blind, you know—or stupid or insensitive! I've driven all the way up here to be with you, and all you do is rush me from dancing to skiing to watching the shooting with Toni and Brandt— anything to prevent us from being alone together. And I want to know why. Have I done something to offend you?"

"Of course not, Jake," Jill said.

"But it doesn't make any sense, Jill," Jake said sharply. "When I arrived up here, you seemed pleased to see me. And now suddenly you're acting as if I've got leprosy. So if I haven't done anything to make you mad, what exactly am I doing that's turning you off?"

"Nothing," Jill said. "You're terrific, Jake. You haven't done anything wrong."

"So you just don't like me anymore, is that it?"

"But I do like you," Jill pleaded. "I like you a lot. If you only knew the way you make me feel, Jake—"

"So what's the problem?"

"The problem is me, I guess," Jill said, turning away from him and wrenching her hands free of his. "I'm scared of getting more involved. I know what you expect from our relationship. You're a grown-up man—you're just not content with kissing me good night!"

"And you don't want us to go any further?"

"I—I don't know. I just don't think I can handle it."

Jake reached out and stroked her cheek. "Look, I know you're straight out of high school, and you've led a sheltered life and all that stuff. I understand. That's why I came up here to be with you. It's so perfect, don't you see? There are no college roommates to pester us. No telephone calls. We're far away from everyone. We can just lock the door and be alone. We can have a fire in the fireplace and be all warm and cozy—doesn't that sound good?"

"Yes," Jill said. "That's the problem. It does sound good."

"But how can that be a problem?"

"It's just the way I've been brought up, I guess," Jill said.

"But you're a big girl now," Jake said. "And Mommy and Daddy are far, far away. You're eighteen, and you can make your own decisions. So it's up to you, Jill. Don't you want to spend the night together?"

"Are you saying you want us to—" Jill paused, unable to say what she knew Jake meant. Her face grew warm, and she couldn't look at him.

"You know what I'm saying, Jill," Jake said firmly. "Don't tell me you haven't thought about it, too."

Jill sighed and met Jake's gaze. "Of course I've thought about it. But I can't, Jake. I really can't."

"Why not?"

"I'd feel so bad about it afterward."

"Why should you feel bad? It's not as if I'm a stranger you've just met. I thought you really cared about me. I know that I care about you. I'm not the sort of guy who goes to bed with any girl he meets. I'm sensitive, too, Jill. I haven't been really involved too often in my life."

Jill looked up at him. "Jake, I really do care about you, and I don't want to hurt you, either. I don't know what I should say to make you understand how I feel."

"I know how you feel. You're scared," Jake said. "But you don't have to be."

"It's not just scared," Jill said. "I'm scared when I have to ski down a steep hill, but I go ahead and do it. It's more than that. It's just the way I am, as a person. I just know that I wouldn't feel right about getting sexually involved with anyone right now. You're right about me—I did have a sheltered childhood. My parents never even talked about sex. They turned off the TV if there was a scene where people started getting undressed. My relationships with boys were all the kind where we kissed and held hands, then went home. I never even had boyfriends like Toni's—you know, the ones she had to fight off in the backseats of cars. I can't shake off my upbringing in two minutes. It's going to take me awhile—"

"You know what I think?" Jake said angrily. "I think you're one of those girls who plays at being helpless and innocent when really she's just a big tease. You didn't exactly stop me when I kissed you, did you? If there's one thing I can't stand, it's a girl who leads you on and then suddenly yells *stop*!"

"But I didn't mean to do that," Jill exclaimed, horrified. "I can't help it if I really like you but I don't want to go to bed with you, can I? I'm sure it's very normal for girls like me not to want to get too involved too quickly."

"If you want the truth," Jake said icily, "it is not normal. Most girls think it's very normal that warm, tender relationships end up with sex. That's what's normal. It's you who's fifty years behind the times. You ought to grow up and realize that you're living in the twentieth century."

"Oh," Jill said as stung by his anger as if he had slapped her face. She turned away so that he wouldn't see the tear that was trickling down her cheek. "I think I'd better go. I'm glad I didn't let you persuade me to do something I didn't want to do, because I can see now that you never cared about me at all. You just wanted to add one more conquest. Someone who cares about another person would never use this sort of pressure."

"You've got it all wrong," Jake yelled. "Someone who cared about another person would want to show it. She wouldn't make feeble little excuses and run home to her mommy. One of these days you're going to find out what life's all about. But it won't be from me!" He turned and stormed out, slamming the door behind him. Jill stood like a statue for a long while, staring at the door. Finally she brushed the tears from her cheeks and let herself quietly out of his room.

TWENTY-ONE

Jill lived through the next few days in a state of shock. She did her work, and she helped Toni hobble around. Mr. Swensen allowed Toni to stay on until Christmas for free. Jill told Toni that Jake had decided to leave, and Toni was tactful enough not to ask any questions. Jill was grateful that Toni didn't press her to talk because she was sure that once she started talking, she would not be able to stop crying. As it was, she tried not to think about Jake or about that horrible scene in his room. She willed herself not to feel anything at all. Most of all, she would not allow herself to think about home. In a few more days it would be Christmas, and she would be home again. But what she really wanted most was to rush straight home, right then. She wanted to feel her father's arms around her and her mother's soft, wispy hair tickling her cheek as she tucked Jill into her own bed. She wanted a cup of hot milk beside her pillow and Teddy Blue nestling into her shoulder.

"But you are not going to rush home," she told herself firmly. "You can't always escape when things go wrong. You've got to learn to stand on your own two feet and get over things. Besides, Toni needs someone to take care of her, at least until she gets used to those crutches."

This last observation was very true. In the past few days since she had gotten her crutches, Toni had already knocked over a large and expensive vase of dried flowers and tripped several guests, as well as almost tumbling down a flight of stairs. Toni seemed to regard her crutches as a pair of wild animals that were impossible to control. When one moved forward, the other shot out sideways, stuck itself between chair legs, or got caught in the carpet. In fact, if Jill hadn't been feeling so depressed, Toni's progress would have been very funny indeed. She would have laughed and made nasty comments, and Toni would have attempted to look proud and annoyed, and they both would have ended up lying on the floor, limp with laughter. But, as it was, Jill could not even manage a smile.

It was especially hard to be feeling depressed right then because the rest of the lodge was getting into the full swing of Christmas. Sleigh rides and Christmas dances had been arranged. Santa was already to be seen wandering through the lobby, handing out candy canes. Jill and several of the other workers had spent an entire day decorating the public areas with pine boughs and holly branches, and the men had just finished putting up an enormous Christmas tree that reached almost to the ceiling.

"You kids have worked hard and done a good job," Mr. Swensen commented. "I think I'll let you decorate the tree for me. You'd like that, wouldn't you?"

The others all seemed excited at the prospect. Jill felt more and more like Scrooge every minute. She stood there, handing up glass balls and paper chains while everyone around her "oohed" and "aahed" and broke into snatches of Christmas carols. She had a strong suspicion that if she opened her mouth she would have said, "Bah, humbug!"

As darkness fell, the workers hurried to put the final touches on the tree in preparation for the official lighting ceremony at six. One of the ski rescue team boys climbed to the top of the ladder and put a huge star in place. Soft Christmas music was piped in over the loudspeaker system. Jill turned away and began efficiently stacking empty boxes to store them away in the housekeeping closet.

"Excuse me, miss, but I have a complaint," a voice said behind her as a finger tapped her angrily on the shoulder. She spun around defensively. "The whole place is full of decorations, and I can't find a single piece of mistletoe," Jake said.

For a long minute she stared at him. "Why would you need mistletoe, sir?" she asked flatly.

"Stupid question," Jake answered, still with no flicker of a smile. "Because I was intending to kiss somebody, and I need an excuse. You see, she might not want to kiss me anymore, so I planned to trap her under the mistletoe. But now there isn't any, so I don't know what to do. Any suggestions?"

His blue eyes looked down at her solemnly.

"You could tell her why you came back," Jill said, her voice quavering slightly. "That would be a start."

"Good idea," he said. "I could tell her that I missed her terribly the moment I drove away. I could tell her that I was just as lonely in the middle of a party as I was there at the cabin, because she wasn't with me. And I could tell her that I was sorry for all the horrible things I said to her—and that I want her back very badly."

"You aren't going to make me change my mind, Jake," Jill said. "I'm still the same person I was when you left."

"I won't try to make you change," Jake said. "I realized as soon as I drove away that I was attracted to you in the first place because you were different. I liked you because you are fresh and innocent, and I don't want you to change, even though it's not going to be easy for me!"

"Oh, Jake," Jill said. "I'm so glad you said that. And I don't intend to live in a convent for the rest of my life. It's just that I'm a late bloomer, I guess, and I need you to be patient with me for a while."

"I'll try very hard," Jake said.

"You see, I realized afterward," Jill explained, "that it wasn't a question of morals or upbringing, really. It was all a question of love. I realized that I'd have to be sure I was really in love before I could commit myself to the kind of relationship you want."

"And do you think," Jake asked, putting his hands on her shoulders and drawing her toward him, "that I should stick around for a while, just in case you could fall in love with a guy like me?"

"I would stick around for a while," Jill whispered. "Because it's very possible."

"Oh, there you are, Jill." Toni's voice interrupted them. "I've been looking all over for you. Where were you?"

"She was busy," Jake said for her. Toni's face, as she focused on Jake for the first time, was a picture of confusion. "What are you doing here? But I thought—gee, I'm sorry, Jill. It looks like I interrupted something."

"It doesn't matter," Jill said, smiling up at Jake. "We have plenty of time."

"You mean you're not planning any more cross-country skiing?" Toni asked.

"No more cross-country skiing," Jill said firmly. "My legs still haven't recovered from the last time. Besides, I've come to the conclusion that skiing is a dangerous sport. After all, look what happened to you!"

"But it was all for a good cause," Toni said smugly.

"What good cause?" Jill asked. "You cannot have gotten the part in the movie, because I'm sure they don't want one-legged skiers."

"That's how much you know," Toni said, beaming like the Cheshire cat. "It so happens that Brandt and his director looked at the rushes of their shooting that day. And one cameraman had had the presence of mind to keep on shooting, all the time I was flying over his head. You can see my terrified face and my skis sailing past. The director says it will be the best action shot in the entire movie!"

"Just as long as they don't lose that piece of film and ask her to repeat that stunt," Brandt said, coming up behind Toni and putting a protective arm around her shoulder. "My nerves could never take going through that a second time. And as for trying to keep her away from further accidents on her crutches—Jill will tell you, Jake, that Toni is a walking, or rather hobbling, time bomb! Thank heavens you've come back to help me get her safely from one place to the next."

"I resent that," Toni said firmly. "You make me sound like an accident-prone maniac. Everyone has trouble controlling their crutches at first!"

"But not everyone goes around wrecking the building and killing other people with their crutches." Brandt laughed.

"I do not," Toni said indignantly. "I can manage them just fine now. And since you all seem to find me so amusing, I'm going over to the window by myself and watch the procession down the mountain."

She turned majestically, tossed back her head, and started to sweep away. Then she looked down at her feet. "Would someone please untangle my crutches from that cable before I bring the entire Christmas tree crashing down," she said frostily.

The others burst out laughing. Soon Toni couldn't help joining them.

"What if I carry you outside so that you can watch the procession?" Brandt asked. "Or are you still too mad at me?"

"I guess I forgive you," Toni said. "After all, I do need a partner for the party tonight, and there aren't all that many cute guys around . . ."

"Oh, I don't know about that," Jill said, smiling.

"Who aren't already taken, I was about to say," Toni finished. Brandt swept her up into his arms and carried her out onto the balcony. Jill and Jake followed. High up on the mountain a tiny string of lights could already be seen zigzagging downward.

"What is this procession?" Jake asked.

"It's the official lighting of the tree," Jill said. "All the ski instructors are coming down with flaming torches, and then Santa is going to throw the switch to turn on the lights."

"Sounds very commercial to me," Jake said.

"But it looks pretty," Jill argued.

Jake nodded. "I have to admit that it does look

pretty." He put his arm around Jill and drew her close to him. The line of lights moved closer and closer. The skiers all had little bells attached to their jackets, and the sound of gentle tinkling echoed from the hills. The combination of the lights and the sound was almost magical. Even though Jill knew that this was something planned by Mr. Swensen and that the skiers were only workers at the lodge, she half expected to see reindeer galloping toward them when the first of the skiers finally reached the bottom of the slope.

Around them everyone was applauding and yelling. A skier dressed as Santa stepped up and threw the switch. Instantly the big tree inside blazed into life, glittering with thousands of tiny white lights that reflected and bounced from silver and gold balls, silver tinsel, and golden chains. The lights reflected out across the snow.

"Come inside, everyone—hot punch on the house," a deep voice shouted. People turned and made for the door. Jake held Jill to him. "Let them go on ahead," he whispered. "I want you to myself for a minute. And you're not going to find any excuses about looking after Toni or having to serve dinner, because I won't listen to them."

Jill lifted her face toward his. "No excuses," she whispered as he began to kiss her.

On Our Own

If you enjoyed reading this book, there are many other series published by Bantam Books which you'll love – SWEET DREAMS, SWEET VALLEY HIGH, CAITLIN, WINNERS, COUPLES and SENIORS. With more on the way – KELLY BLAKE, SWEPT AWAY and SWEET VALLEY TWINS – how can you resist!

These books are all available at your local bookshop or newsagent, though should you find any difficulty in obtaining the books you would like, you can order direct from the publisher, at the address below. Also, if you would like to know more about the series, or would simply like to tell us what you think of the series, write to:

Kim Prior,
On Our Own,
Transworld Publishers Ltd.,
61–63 Uxbridge Road,
Ealing,
London W5 5SA.

To order books, please list the title(s) you would like, and send together with a cheque or postal order made payable to TRANSWORLD PUBLISHERS LTD. Please allow the cost of the book(s) plus postage and packing charges as follows:

All orders up to a total of £5.00   50p
All orders in excess of £5.00   Free

Please note that payment must be made in pounds sterling; other currencies are unacceptable.

(The above applies to readers in the UK and Republic of Ireland only)

If you live in Australia or New Zealand, and would like more information about the series, please write to:

Sally Porter,
On Our Own,
Transworld Publishers (Aust) Pty Ltd.,
15–23 Helles Avenue,
Moorebank,
N.S.W. 2170,
AUSTRALIA

Kiri Martin,
On Our Own,
c/o Corgi and Bantam Books New Zealand,
Cnr. Moselle and Waipareira Avenues,
Henderson,
Auckland,
NEW ZEALAND

KELLY BLAKE: TEEN MODEL

KELLY BLAKE
She's A Star

Meet 16-year-old Kelly Blake, tall and beautiful. Watch her rise in the glamorous world of high fashion. Share the excitement as Kelly is discovered and begins her career as a top model. Share her hopes and her fears as she juggles her growing career, the demands of school commitments, *and* the need for time just to be herself, Kelly Blake, sixteen, pretty, and in love with the boy next door.

Catch a Star on the Rise!

LOOK FOR:

DISCOVERED!
KELLY BLAKE: TEEN MODEL No. 1

RISING STAR
KELLY BLAKE: TEEN MODEL No. 2

HARD TO GET
KELLY BLAKE: TEEN MODEL No. 3

HEADLINERS
KELLY BLAKE: TEEN MODEL No. 4

And don't forget to watch for more KELLY BLAKE books coming soon.

TRUE LOVE!   CRUSHES!   BREAKUPS!   MAKEUPS!

Find out what it's like to be a COUPLE.

Ask your bookseller for any titles you have missed:

Coming soon . . .

COUPLES SPECIAL EDITION
SUMMER HEAT!